A Grief Well Ended

a novel by

Erica Kinsey

To Sally -
A new but
wonderful friend!
Erica Kinsey
(Freddie)

This is a work of fiction. All resemblence to characters, living or dead, are purely coincidental. Only the events mentioned are real and a part of the American history.

ISBN: 0-7596-5541-3

This book is printed on acid free paper.

1stBooks – rev. 11/21/01

Dedicated to my children,
Drew and Robert

Acknowledgements

Grateful thanks to Drew, who always displayed interest in World War II; to Leonora DeMaio who read the manuscript for accuracy and speech patterns, and to the staff of the Granby, CT library who provided needed assistance on several occasions.

Chapter One

Tonight we will have fireworks after Brentley's Fourth of July parade and our family picnic. I've grown used to this annual American celebration and enjoy the unvaried events. Although I am English, I can appreciate the fervor behind this most patriotic of all American holidays, especially since my husband is a retired History professor.

We are old now, married more than fifty years, Still loving, but no longer lovers; memories sustain us rather than shared passion; friends and companions, fortunate to have found each other in the aftermath of World War II.

As I begin to dice potatoes for the salad, my thoughts drift back. The century has turned. All too often present-memories elude me, but I can still recall the amazement I felt when I met with a supercilious British Intelligence officer in London in September 1945 and found out my lover whom I had thought lost to me forever still lived. Once again, I felt the anger at the cruel deception that had taken place all those years ago.

I stared at Colonel Jenkins in absolute astonishment, the words he had just spoken beyond belief. "But," I stammered, "I was told Dan had died in a plane crash right after its takeoff. What happened? Why was I told this?"

The colonel shuffled a few papers on his desk, cleared his throat then looked directly into my eyes. "Mrs.—er—Ferguson, I'm truly sorry. That was a necessary wartime security measure, both for his sake and yours."

"But it's September 1945. The European war has been over since May. Why am I just being told now that he's still alive? Where is he? I think I deserve the truth in this matter." I knew tears were about to fill my eyes, but I was determined to show no weakness in front of this man. "My whole life was changed with this lie!"

"Let me try to explain—"

"I doubt that any explanation will be satisfactory!" I replied heatedly, aware of the fact I would have liked to wipe that superior, condescending smile from Jenkin's face. I had had to wait until late afternoon to see him and the interview was at his request, not mine. I had been summoned to London without a by-your-leave.

Aware of my fury, he hesitated for a second then said quietly, "I realize you were both in love and intended to marry. At that time we were made aware of an information leak that placed both of your lives in jeopardy. You had a very important mission to accomplish, as you well know, and it was essential that we protect it at all costs. You *know* this to be true, Mrs. Ferguson," he admonished me, waiting for me to nod my reluctant assent to his statement. "We also had information that Mr. Childress had been linked to your name in Gestapo files. We believed the only way to provide cover was—to eliminate you both by adding your names to a Pan-American Clipper manifest—and having the plane crash at sea, thus causing— ahem—the demise of you both."

Jenkins sighed, hesitated again, seeking I knew the best way to cover what I now realized was a grave bureaucratic error, grave as it affected me, of little import to the powers-to-be. "As you may know, your superior passed away two years later when you were living in Fleetford and had resigned from service. On a need-to-know basis, you weren't notified of your superior's passing, and unfortunately he left no—notation for us to contact you and explain the matter."

I stared at Jenkins coldly, knowing there never would have been any notation. Most pertinent information had been kept in the man's head, not on paper. Especially in my case.

Aloud, I asked Colonel Jenkins exactly why I had been requested to appear before him. Certainly not because British Intelligence wanted to apologize for an oversight on their part. Not likely at all. I was totally amazed when Jenkins began to explain I was being asked to meet with Dan in America on a postwar mission in service to His Majesty, should I decide to do so.

Dear God! "I don't know where he lives!" I exclaimed. "I think it was someplace in the eastern United States, near New York." When we parted we didn't exchange addresses. That wasn't quite true—he had given me an accommodation address in New York City, a post office box probably long-since cancelled.

"We've located him. Now, this is what we need done." Jenkins slipped an enlarged photograph from a manila folder. "Do you recognize or remember this man?"

I gazed at the photograph trying to place where I had seen him. It certainly had to be at the beginning of the war five years ago. I knew the face—but from where? It was a handsome, blond Nordic type, half-smile, half-closed eyes, a slightly contemptuous expression on his face, a scar crossing his left cheek. Suddenly I knew who he was: The driver of the vehicle the French resistance group had chosen to drive Dan and I and the Professor to the tiny landing field used by Britain to fly prisoners or escapees out of Europe. The man who had betrayed us. But as the driver he had been all wit and charm, not the sort of man he appeared to be in the photo. I told Jenkins yes, I could identify him, and proceeded to do so. Could I name him? I was not sure, I couldn't remember if he had ever told us. It was unlikely he would have, given the times we were in, or it would have been an alias to protect himself. Then I suddenly recalled later my superior had referred to him as Dieter, but no surname was ever mentioned.

"Very good. Excellent." The first words of approval I had heard from Jenkins who, I realized, had no use for female operatives in the intelligence service, and certainly not for Joan Poynton Ferguson. "We want you to fly over to the States, meet with Mr. Childress and determine if he can verify your identification. My secretary is trying to reach Childress by transatlantic telephone and when she does, you may speak to him. You understand, of course, there will be no cost to you. His

Majesty's government will pay any expenses connected with the trip, but there will be no personal renumeration As you remember, we have—ah—accepted certain expenses of yours in the past." I nodded again, knowing what he said was true.

We sat in silence, waiting for the overseas connection to be made. I wondered what I would say to Dan.

"Does Mr. Childress know I'm alive?" I asked and when Jenkins shook his head, I tried to believe I could convince someone I thought lost to me forever that I was who I was. It would have been easier if we could have spoken to each other alone without the presence of Jenkins, but this was clearly not to be.

As we waited I looked out the window at water traffic on the Thames. Across the river I could see piles of rubble and the long necks of mechanized cranes moving over the wreckage of buildings destroyed during the bombing raids. London had survived, as had England, but even in victory life would be hard for Britons for some years to come. There were shortages of everything: food, machinery, clothing, and it was difficult to rejoice in peace when there was so little to brighten our lives. I hadn't been able to find but one or two items on my worn piece of paper which contained a running list of necessities not available in my rural village.

"I must state that we want this matter discussed as soon as possible, Mrs. Ferguson." Jenkin's high-pitched public school voice interrupted my thoughts. I nodded, commenting that I needed a few days to make arrangements and to search for some clothing. Five years of war had created shreds out of my wardrobe and I was at a loss to assemble even one or two outfits that would see me through the trip and perhaps a week in America.

"Ah, perhaps we could fund whatever clothing you might need for the trip. We realize a rural housewife might need to purchase a few things." Despite the disparaging remark I saw a twinkle in the Colonel's eyes. He evidently realized the way to a woman's heart was by providing clothing on her back, so to speak.

"That's very kind of you, Colonel. I imagine I will have to take advantage of your kind offer," I replied stiffly.

The phone finally rang. My heart began to beat rapidly, a variety of emotions swirled through my mind, anticipation, fear and longing to hear Dan's voice again. Jenkins picked it up, listened intently for a second, then handed it to me, announcing "Your party's on the line."

I thought it was before noon in America. For an instant I could only hear the pounding of my heart in my ear, then I cleared my throat and said, "Hello, Dan? This is Joan Poynton speaking. How are you?" Not the most original opening and I know my voice was shaking.

There was a brief silence, accompanied by light static, then I heard Dan's baritone voice—could I fail to recognize it?— replying, "There must be some mistake or you've reached the wrong party. Joan Poynton is deceased."

I was totally in thrall hearing him speak. I would have remembered the timbre of his voice in the grave. "No, Dan, this is Joan Poynton. There's been a terrible misunderstanding. It truly is I."

"If this is someone's idea of a joke, I'm not amused." His voice was cold and I feared he would hang up. How could I convince him? "Dan, it's Cupcake." I heard him inhale sharply when I used the foolish endearment he had called me years ago. I didn't dare look at Colonel Jenkins who was probably aghast at my method of identification. Nervously, I continued.

"I have to see you, Dan, on official business and I'll try to explain everything. Are you free to see me on-"I named the date on the note the Colonel pushed across the desk. "I will fly to New York on September 21. You're living in" I glanced down again, "Connecticut. That's near New York?"

"Right next to New York," I could hear slight amusement in his voice. "Why don't you cable me your ETA and flight and I'll meet you at LaGuardia."

5

I had heard of Connecticut, but was it a state, city or region? I couldn't remember. But I didn't want to have to cope with right-hand-side-of-the-road driving. "Thank you, Dan. I'll do that. Dan, I look forward so to seeing you again." That was the understatement of the century I thought. We were disconnected, probably by Jenkin's secretary, in the interest of economy.

"Well, that went very nicely," commented the Colonel who had been monitoring the conversation. "I assume you'll be able to make suitable arrangements at home."

"I'll manage, I'm sure," I replied coolly. Reaching for my worn leather handbag I rose and turned toward the door. The Colonel was there before me, opening the door quickly for me.

As I started to leave he touched my shoulder and amazed me by saying in what I believed to be all sincerity, "His Majesty's government thanks you, Mrs. Ferguson. I am personally pleased you will have an opportunity to be with Mr. Childress again." He handed me an envelope explaining this was a chit to be handed to a certain buyer at Harrod's who would seek to obtain such items as I might deem necessary for my journey.

"I will have all the necessary documents you will need delivered to your home within twenty-four hours."

It seemed simpler to stay in town and make the purchases I would need than to return home. I decided I would call Catherine, my mother-in-law, to tell her I would not return that evening, but I would explain all when I arrived in Fleetford the next afternoon. As I dined alone in the hotel dining room I enjoyed contemplating the items I would need to purchase and wondered if British Intelligence would mind if I bought a few linens for my cottage. I suspected they would!

I was exhausted, but tired as I was, my thoughts drifted back to my brief conversation with Dan. What would it be like to meet him again, after half a decade? Would he have changed much from the quick-witted, audacious young man I had loved? Even now, recalling the sound of his voice, I dwelt on the memory of his face, the remembrance of his embraces—the memories I had tried so hard to subdue now overwhelming me with a flood of emotion like the surge of an ocean tide.

How could I explain to him what had been done to us? And—I would have to tell him about my marriage to John. But I would not tell him about our son. Not yet.

Chapter Two

When I arrived in Fleetford, I was relieved to find my bicycle where I left it, outside the stationmaster's office, padlocked to a rack. Transportation was still a terrible problem in England; gas was expensive and not easy to obtain. I unlocked it, placed my parcels in the twin baskets over the rear wheels, slung my purse over my shoulder and proceeded to pedal the half-mile to my cottage.

I lived with my mother-in-law in a tiny cottage just outside of the village. Johnny, my son, and I shared a little bedroom under the eves, hot in the summer, cold in the winter. The cottage was on the property of a larger home still owned by family, but presently requisitioned for government facilities. We anticipated it being turned back for our use, but no time had been set. The main house was Georgian in style, built of the lovely golden stone used extensively during the eighteenth and nineteenth centuries. It was sheltered by hundred-year old trees whose leaf-laden branches provided shadowed coolness in the summer and bare, buffered cruel winds blowing down from the Scottish highlands in the winter.

Catherine, slender, grey-haired, tranquil and self-possessed at fifty-two, came out of the house to greet me, smiling as I leaned the bicycle up against the garden shed. "You look like a schoolgirl still," she complimented me. "Whatever have your purchased?

"Wait till you see," I smiled. "Where's Johnny?"

"Napping. I put him down after lunch. He should be up shortly"

"Then let's talk out here." I led her to two dilapidated lawnchairs, badly needing paint. It was still warm enough in the golden afternoon sunshine to enjoy the garden.

Catherine listened intently as I told her what I could of the government request I fly to America to identify an individual I had met in France, before its fall.

"But why you?" she asked in bewilderment.

I knew my answer might open up a kettle of worms, but I had decided to be as forthright as possible since no mention had been made of national security by the pompous Colonel Jenkins. "Because before the war I worked for British Intelligence. I was stationed in Paris."

Catherine's eyes widened. "A spy?"

"Well, I think it was called operational liaison."

"But you were so young," she protested. "A mere girl."

"There were exceptional circumstances. At the time I was sent there because of people I had known through my father." I shook my head. "I can't say anymore, Catherine, not at this point in time." I told her I would be receiving documents soon, but I could not promise to tell her anymore. I explained I would be flying out next week and would likely be gone no more than a few days.

"Do you think it has anything to do with the war criminal trials in Nuremberg?"

I suspected it did, but shook my head and told her I didn't know. To avoid further question I suggested we open my bundles and view my purchases.

After I showed her what I had brought for my trip, a grey worsted ready-made suit, the obligatory little black dress—my prewar one was turning green—a sweater set and two blouses, plus some desperately needed underwear and black pumps, I handed her a package. "For you, Catherine." With my own money I had purchased a twin-set in a lovely shade of rose and woolen yard goods to make a matching skirt. I never could have obtained it without my note to the Harrod's buyer. Tears came to Catherine's eyes. The war had depleted her wardrobe as well as mine.

I showed her the few items I had been able to find for Johnny. I also pleased her with the purchase of four sheets and three bath towels, desperately needed by the linen press. "What riches," she sighed.

9

My final purchase was a luscious fruitcake from Harrod's which we would sample at teatime.

"Mummy!" My son Johnny came racing out of the house. Fair-haired, freckled, forehead and nose like mine, I could see Dan's mouth and set of chin in his face. I wondered how I could think of leaving him for a week and prayed the plane would deliver me safely to the States and back again. At that moment I regretted my agreement to visit Dan. Or did I?

I hugged Johnny and gave him the one present I could find, a small cast-iron train engine. He went over the walkway to make those endearing little-boy noises to indicate the engine was actively working. Catherine and I shared a smile at his intense absorption in his play. Like everything else, toys were in short supply, especially in our little village.

That evening, lying in the bed I had shared with my deceased husband and on which in secret I had wept over the loss of Dan, I remembered the events which led up to the adventure I would shortly undertake. Since London I had had no time to think back on those days in Paris shortly before Hitler's blitzkrieg had shattered so many lives, including Dan's and mine. But now I could not help remembering everything in sharp, poignant detail.

Chapter Three

My memories returned to Paris l940, just days before the Nazi divisions entered the city. Most foreigners had already escaped Paris. I was under orders to stay until I made contact with a certain physics professor whose input British Intelligence deemed essential to future armament operations. I knew his name, I had a current bad photograph, a cover story which would account for my still being in the country and a contact who might or might not be still available, given the current crisis alert. I was twenty-two years old, terrified, uncertain what to do next.

I remembered standing at my hotel room door struggling with a key which seemed to be the wrong one for the door. Beside me was my suitcase, a small handbag and a briefcase filled with the documents supposedly to be delivered to the professor; innocuous, I had been told, no danger of compromising my cover story. Earlier that day I had reached his office at the Sorbonne and been told to try to reach him late in the afternoon. It was now quarter-to-four and I would miss him if I could not get to the telephone in my room within a very few minutes.

"Let me try, miss." I heard a pleasant male American voice at my elbow and glanced down to see a hand outstretched toward mine, ready to make an attempt to unlock the door.

I was grateful for the offer and murmured in exasperation, "I don't think they've given me the right key, but, please, if you can open it I will be so grateful."

A couple of turns back and forth and the knob responded. "Here, let me show you what to do so you can manage it next time yourself.."

I felt foolish. It was simpler than I thought. I turned to thank the voice and was surprised to see a tall, smiling young man gazing down into my eyes. I thanked him but rejected his offer to carry my sparse luggage inside. "There's no need. I can manage." Attractive though he was, I had no intention of beginning a flirtation in the midst of my efforts to complete my assignment.

"I wouldn't unpack much," he advised. "I really think you should consider getting out of France within the next forty-eight hours. The U.S. Embassy has already warned their citizens to find transportation out of the country as soon as they can."

He was right, of course, and I felt a chill penetrate my stomach as I listened to his words.

"I'm going as soon as I can locate an old friend of my father's. He's an elderly gentleman and I'm terribly concerned about his safety."

"Maybe I can help you. The sooner you find your friend, the sooner you can get out of here. How about dinner tonight?"

"I'm not certain what my plans are," I answered hastily, thinking it best to avoid any further involvement.

"Well," he gestured down the hall. "My room's down there, No. 217. I'll check back with you around six o'clock. We could at least have a drink at the bar."

Maybe I could sneak out of my room before then and evade his very persistent advances, although if times had not been what they were I would have been inclined to encourage him. He was very attractive, I noticed, and seemed to be friendly, like most Americans, but not aggressive. His concern struck me as genuine, but I couldn't afford any involvement whatsoever. "Perhaps—we'll see what transpires." I slipped into my room, hastily closed the door, anxious to make my telephone call.

"Professor Aubuchon has already left for the day and I'm not sure when he will return," the operator informed me in highly accented English. I had a feeling she wanted to say he was gone for good. She refused to give me his home address, but did relent and give me a telephone number where I might be able to reach him. I thanked her, hung up, and immediately called. After a few rings, a woman's voice answered and told me the professor had not reached home yet, but was expected very soon.

In my inadequate school-girl French I explained that I was the daughter of an old friend of his who would like me to give him a message from my father before I left the country. Yes, it was quite urgent. I could be reached at my hotel, but I would call back in fifteen minutes to see if he had arrived home yet. I left my name and wondered how I would ever be able to reach him in time to explain my government's plan to extricate him before the Nazis overran France and took him to Germany.

The cover story was quite close to the truth. I remembered spending a summer in the early Thirties with the professor and his wife who were guests in my parent's seaside cottage. I recalled them as being remotely kind to my sister and I, but not adults who enjoyed the company of children. Daily, the professor and my father spent much time closeted in the study, but I was too young to be the least bit interested in their discussions. I could remember his face clearly, thin with sharp, high cheekbones, dark eyes, bushy eyebrows and what I would now describe as wariness or anxiety in his manner of viewing the world and its occupants. Occasionally he would take us to the beach to play in the sand or at the ocean's edge, but there was no warmth whatsoever in his treatment of us. He was remote, vigilant against accident, but we knew we really weren't people in his eyes. Not even little people.

My mother cautioned us to be polite, not to annoy the Aubuchons, and to stay out of our father's study at all times. The last was easy. We didn't care about the pile of folders, scraps of paper, charts and tabulations spread helter-skelter over the oversized table which served as Father's desk. The end of summer came, we returned after the bank holidays, and never heard from the Aubuchons again. I had to dredge through many childhood memories before I could recall their presence in that long ago prewar summer.

The second time I called I was successful. I asked the professor if he recalled the summer he spent at Dr. Poynton's summer place near Brighton. He answered affirmatively, but with careful hesitation. Did he recall the two children he occasionally watched at the water's edge? Dead silence.

Finally, "Yes, I believe so. Sarah, and the youngest girl was Joan—Joan Elizabeth. Nice children."

"Well, this is Joan Elizabeth speaking, Professor Aubuchon. I would like to visit you this evening before I leave. I have papers for you from my father that might be of great interest to you. They concern the properties of argon." Whatever that was. But that was what I was told to say to identify myself to the professor.

I heard him draw his breath in sharply, then he calmly invited me to join him that evening for a late supper at eight-thirty.

"Could we possible meet an hour earlier, Professor. Would that be too inconvenient for your wife?" Now that I had located him, I wanted to settle matters as soon as possible.

"My wife passed away, Joan Elizabeth. It will be just you and I." I heard the sadness in his voice and wondered how recently she had died, but didn't want to ask.

I jotted down the directions as he gave them to me and wondered how I would find a car to drive me there. There was little if no transportation in the city. Everything with wheels had been commandeered by the government or purchased at exorbitantly high prices by those who sought refuge in the countryside. The attractive young American? Perhaps he had access to something. Plus he probably was a more competent driver. I had been driving for little more than six months and those were on small lanes in rural England.

It was now five-thirty and I had to arrange something as quickly as possible. I was told nothing was available in every phone call I made. The city had been stripped of almost all mechanized transportation. Did they have any suggestions? Get to the airport and take any flight out, to anywhere, that would get me away from France. What in heaven's name was I going to do?

I heard a soft rap on the door and hoped it would be my new American friend. He stood there smiling and asked me if I had come to any decision about dinner.

"Yes," I responded. "I'd very much enjoy your company tonight." Could he wait while I freshened up? I'd been making a few phone calls trying to locate my father's friend. Yes, I had finally reached him. Then I suddenly realized I didn't know my new friend's name. (Nor did he know mine, I thought.) We introduced ourselves and after a touch of powder and lipstick on my part, I gathered my purse and briefcase and walked to the cranky hotel lift, thinking to myself if we got stuck between floors on the way down there would be no one left in the city who could repair it and rescue us. I saw the quizzical expression on Dan's face as he eyed my briefcase, but he asked no questions.

What, I asked over dinner, was he doing in France at such a precarious time. Hadn't he, like I, been warned to leave the country as soon as possible?

"Yes, but I'm a very minor functionary at the U.S. Embassy and as such I have to hang around until we're all evacuated, or flown out, or whatever they decide to do." Did he know the city well?

"I can get around."

Did he have a car at his command? (I held my breath waiting for his answer.)

"I can get one. Do you need to go somewhere?"

I explained that I wanted to reach my father's friend to give him papers that might aid in his research, even though the impending war might interrupt his on-going progress.

"Do they concern the properties of argon?" Dan asked quietly as I stared at him, appalled at his question, not knowing how to reply. Was he really a US government employee or, God forbid, a Nazi spy? Had I walked right into a trap? Why, oh, why had British Intelligence entrusted an inexperienced twenty-two year old with this mission? .

"It's too bad Professor Aubuchon couldn't see you at eight o'clock," Dan continued in a low voice. "We'll have to eat fast to make it by seven-thirty."

I quickly understood his comments were to tell me he was aware of my mission. I had not mentioned the professor's name at any time. "How did you know about Professor Aubuchon's interest in argon research?" I questioned cautiously.

"I've heard it mentioned around the Embassy. The professor is a world-renowned expert, or so I've been told by higher-ups." Much later he told me Aubuchon had checked with the US Embassy regarding my bona-fides.

"And are you also a physicist?" I questioned.

He shook his head, saying no more. Glancing at his watch he said, "We'd better forget supper. It's six-thirty and I have to walk back to the Embassy to pick up the car. I didn't dare drive it here and leave it parked on the street."

I gathered up my purse, briefcase and arose. He was right. We had little time to waste, though I was hungry. Dan asked the waiter for the bill and also for a pastry to take with us. The waiter frowned, probably thinking we had no proper appreciation of French cuisine.

The light was dimming as we left and, glancing around, Dan shook his head and asked if I could manage a three-block walk. "I don't like leaving you here alone. Are those shoes comfortable enough to manage?" I told him yes, and glanced around myself trying to see if there was a face I had seen before during the day or prior to entering the restaurant. The only one I recognized was Dan's and though he seemed to be what he said he was, I was nervous about his sudden appearance and knowledge of the professor and I.

We were certainly noticed by the passers-by. A couple of women gazed at Dan with interest and a few men looked at me. It was obvious we weren't French from our dress and more than one person wondered what two foreign young people were doing there when the collapse of France seemed imminent.

"Smile, Joan," I heard Dan say and the next thing I knew he had his hand on my shoulder holding me close by his side as we walked along. "Everyone loves a lover," he reminded me. "We'll look less suspicious this way."

At one point we stopped and he gazed into my eyes, then leaned down to kiss me, murmuring, "Hug me back." I tightened my arms around his neck and proceeded to cooperate with all the enthusiasm I could muster, not an effort, I must admit. His body was solid, his arms held me tightly against him and firm, warm lips encouraged my complete cooperation. We were both conscious of our sudden overwhelming response to one another as our breath quickened in response to our closeness. As we approached the US Embassy he backed me up against a wrought-iron fence and proceeded to kiss me again. This time I endeavored to make my response a little less ardent.

"Relax," he breathed in my ear. "This is the benefit of someone watching us from that five-storey apartment house across the street. Look on the third floor, left side."

He adroitly turned my body sideways so I could see. A brief glimpse of someone, then the sudden movement of drapes as whoever stepped behind them, out of sight. I nodded my head, then reached up again to bring his face down to mine.

Just before we kissed I saw him grin. "If this is what secret agents do, I'm planning a full-time career." He felt me stiffen at his comment, but before I could react to his remark he took me by the arm and we strolled up to the embassy gate guarded by a uniformed man from one branch of the American services, but which one I couldn't be sure. I was also unable to hear what Dan said to him, but after a minute we were allowed to enter.

A Ford sedan drove up to us, Dan helped me into the car and changed places with the driver. Surely a German spy would have no means of commandeering a car from the U.S. Embassy pool, but I decided I would try to determine exactly what role this young man was playing. I drew in my breath and turned to Dan to ask, "How are you involved in this? What do you know you're not telling me?"

"What are you not telling me?" Dan countered. "We're both on the same side, even though the United States hasn't entered the war."

"Begin by proving to me you're who you say you are. Doesn't the Embassy issue identification?"

He reached into his inside jacket pocket, handed me a folder with his passport and a small identification card stating he was attached to the American embassy, both documents embossed with the Great Seal of the United States of America. To me they looked authentic, but such items could be forged and obtained on the black market. I remember noticing that he lived in Connecticut and that he was born in 1914, making him four years older than me. "All right, who do you report to besides the ambassador? Some under-person?"

"I'm the liaison between our Major Everett and General Barclay whom I believe you know." His eyes were on the road filled with slow-moving vehicles and refugees on foot, but he must have seen me start at the mention of General Barclay's name, my immediate supervisor and close friend of my deceased father. It was at that point I realized I could relax in the presence of a friendly agent. Dan continued, "Do you believe me enough now to tell me why Professor Aubuchon is so important that British Intelligence would send in a young woman to try to bring him to England?" I was immediately annoyed by what I felt was a disparaging tone in his voice.

"Because the young woman is the only one who knows what he looks like," I replied tartly. "Is that reason enough? Now, are you going to explain why you're here with me?"

"At your General Barclay's request. He realized that things have changed drastically since he met with you three weeks ago. I'm here to lend a hand, but it's your operation." He gave me a quick, mock salute with his right hand. "I'm here to give you cover. Kisses any time we seem to be in danger. We can practise if you like, just to make certain we're getting it right."

I frowned at him. "I don't think that will be necessary," I replied primly. Then I ruined the effect by giggling.

H reached across my back and squeezed my shoulder lightly. "You never know," he assured me.

Were all Americans this flippant? Flirtatious? Confident of their appeal? I enjoyed the warmth of his hand for a second then removed it, leaning forward to try to identify where we were. "I don't think it's much further along. We passed one of the landmarks right back there." I was looking for a street that ran the far side of a tall, grey-stoned Gothic type structure mentioned by the professor. "There, Dan. Turn left."

Half-way down the block from the professor's house was a disabled touring car, its right tyre flat. I didn't give it a second glance, but Dan slowed down beside it, stopped, got out and peered inside, calling out in English, "Anyone inside? Can I be of help?" He checked the backseat, then climbed back into our car again, turning it around and backing into the driveway running alongside the professor's house. I knew he was suspicious we had been followed and credited him with astute judgment.

I searched the face of the older man who opened the door when we knocked. "You're late," he commented and the voice assured me he was still the same individual who had reluctantly taken care of two little girls at times during that long-ago vacation. "Joan—," he let me supply my second name, possibly as a check, possibly because he wasn't sure what to call the adult woman in front of him. "Joan Elizabeth," I announced firmly. "And this is my associate, Daniel Childress. May we come in?"

The dining room table was lit by two or three candles. It was so dim at first I couldn't see the identical briefcase to mine laying on a corner of the table. Beside it was a worn raincoat. No suitcase. Nothing else to mark his life for the past decade or so in France. A slight breeze stirred the heavy drapes and brought the scent of some night-blooming flower into the room.

Professor Aubuchon gestured toward the food and advised us to eat something before we left. I made cheese sandwiches for all of us, added the wrapped pastry the scornful waiter at the restaurant had given us and poured small glasses of wine. It was Dan who raised his glass to a toast "to success." I wondered if that would prove to be a jinx in the hours to come.

I heard a noise from the front of the house and moved behind the curtain to see if anyone was there. I saw two men standing by the embassy car, looking to see if by any chance the keys were still in the ignition. At the wave of my hand Dan looked out and bellowed at them to leave the car alone. In accented, but more than passable French I noticed.

"We'd better get going," he urged as I gathered up the Professor's briefcase. Just before we closed the front door I saw him glance around the parlor once more and thought I saw a glint of tears in his eyes. He was probably thinking of his wife, I surmised. How many lives all over France and Europe were being torn apart at this moment I wondered.

Chapter Four

Before starting the engine we sat while Dan questioned me as to what story we would use, should we be stopped by whomever. I told him I was Professor Aubuchon's English niece. His sister married my father's brother, Philip Poynton. I had documents to prove it as well as tickets for the Lisbon flight from Orly airport at eight o'clock the next morning. In reality, I explained, we were to cut off before the airport and drive to a remote area behind an ancient monastery where the land was just flat enough to allow a small plane to land and take off.

"Then that's where I'll take you," Dan stated. "You're sure of the directions?"

"Yes. You sound like a husband, not that I've ever been married." I glanced over at him. He was grinning at my remark and answered, "Just checking."

We had gone maybe two miles when Dan slowed down. Ahead was a group of soldiers searching cars. French soldiers, I thought.

"Better let me do the talking, Cupcake," he cautioned. "Get your identification out. They're going to ask for it." From then on, it was an irate, impatient, typical American who spoke. "What's going on? Why are you stopping me and my friends? I'm an American citizen. You have no right to detain us!"

I easily slipped into the role of an indignant visitor. "This gentlemen is driving my uncle and me to to Orly airport. I have tickets for tomorrow morning's Lisbon flight but we thought we'd better get there tonight, rather than chance missing the flight."

I handed over our identification and, reluctantly, the airplane tickets. They were closely examined by two men, and retained while the officer spoke to us.

"The flight has been cancelled. You will have to return to your home or hotel. Call the airport when you return and ask if a new time has been set for departure. Turn your car around now. There is a barricade ahead and you can't go beyond this point."

More indignant protests by Dan and me. The professor sat quietly in the back of car, avoiding any verbal interchange. The man who had been checking our credentials glanced at him and asked his name, but the professor merely shook his head and touched his ear to indicate he could not hear.

"My uncle is profoundly deaf," I explained. Could I answer any questions for them? The man said no, evidently losing interest in his query. He stepped aside and motioned for us to go back, returning our tickets. We had no choice and Dan reversed the car in a quick display of righteous anger then proceeded back in the direction of the capital.

"What now?" the professor asked. Good question. I looked at Dan and asked, "Do you want to take a chance on finding a side road paralleling this?" I opened the glove box and searched for a map. Nothing. Did everyone in the American embassy always know exactly where they were going?

"Maybe we'd better find a telephone and call the airport. They may check to make certain we're concerned about missing that flight," Dan advised.

"We? I only have two tickets."

"That's an editorial 'we.' I can't leave with you. I'm only supposed to make certain you both get on the real flight. Someone else will be delighted to have your seats when you don't show up."

"Dan, will you have to stay after the Germans get to Paris?"

He recognized the concern in my voice and reached over to take my hand for a second, squeezing it lightly. "I don't know, Cupcake. But I want your phone number before you leave. We'll catch up with each other later on, I promise."

I was certain this was just a line, but hoped maybe we would meet again. I knew I was more and more attracted to this young American, though a part of me chalked it up to wartime urgency. We were both young and no one who hadn't lived through that period in history would ever know the sense of immediate

22

attraction and desire fueled by awareness of the brief time couples had to establish a relationship. It was too easy to slip into commitment and consummation of what in peacetime would have been a mere flirtation. I was too level-headed, too cautious, too sensible to allow myself to be led by emotion. I couldn't afford to. Not now, not with the responsibility for the safe conduct of Professor Aubuchon to England on my hands. Or so I told myself.

We drove back to Paris in silence, both Dan and I trying to decide what the next best move would be. We drew up in front of the American embassy, passed through the gate where Dan presented his identification again and was directed to park on the side of the building.

"You can call the airport from here while I speak to my superior," Dan instructed. "Getting out of here may be a problem. I'm sure the Embassy is under constant surveillance." One more challenge in an almost impossible assignment, one that seemed doomed from the beginning, probably largely to my inexperience. "We'll worry about it when the time comes." So far I had been impressed by Dan's quick-witted resourcefulness and realized I would have been lost without his help.

The professor and I were left waiting outside of Major Everett's office. I was told I could use the desk phone to call the airport to check on the flight status while we waited. The Frenchman had been right. The early morning flight had been cancelled. I was advised to call back at nine o'clock the next morning to get further information. It was eight-forty-five as I spoke and I realized we had only five hours to meet the scheduled landing at the tiny airstrip of the plane which would take the professor and I back to England.

Through this whole period of time the professor had said less than a dozen words to me. I couldn't decide if he were highly anxious, or simply didn't care. He probably thought I was an incompetent idiot. "Don't worry," I tried to assure him. "We'll make it somehow."

He surprised me by smiling and saying, "I have utmost faith in you, Joan Elizabeth, and your American friend."

"You have all the necessary information Britain needs?" I had visions of having to return to his home for a vital piece of paper.

He patted his worn briefcase. "In here, but before we leave, I think I'll give you a copy of the basics, in case anything happens." He opened his case and handed me a small oilskin pouch tightly stuffed with papers, long strings attached so that I could wrap it around my waist. I was afraid to leave him to ask for a loo from the guard outside the door, so I walked to a corner, turned my back, slipped my blouse from my skirt and tied the pouch securely around my waist. Rearranging my clothing, I turned around to see Dan grinning at me.

"If you'd waited, I'd have been glad to help," he assured me.

"I managed without difficulty," I replied tartly. I returned to the problem of how to get to our two o'clock rendezvous with the British airplane. "How about an ambulance?" I wondered aloud. "Would there still be any in Paris? Wouldn't they send one to the American Embassy? One of us would have to be the patient, maybe I could be the nurse and we'd need an attendant or a doctor."

Dan considered the suggestion thoughtfully. "It might work. The professor would have to do the talking, neither of us could pass for French, Joan. I guess that makes you the nurse and I'll be the patient. Appendicitis, I think. I can groan in English—no one will know the difference."

His flippancy made me smile as I questioned, "How do we get an ambulance?"

"Leave that to me. I'll go find Major Everett and see what he can do for us."

After Dan had gone in search of the major I turned to the Professor and asked. "Do you think you can manage this? Are you willing to try? I can think of no other way to get us out of here. I'm not certain there's any medical facility near the monastery, unless you know of one."

"There's a private tuberculosis clinic run by the Sisters of Mercy in that general area." He paused. "Maybe we could say there was a surgeon there who said he would operate if we got there by tomorrow morning." That would provide an explanation for the authorities, I thought, if we had to convince them our need for haste was urgent and legitimate. "I'm pretty sure I can convince anyone who stops us I'm a doctor," Professor Aubuchon added, "I had two years of premedical courses before I switched to physics."

"Looks like you're going to be the one to save us," I commented. "It's supposed to be the other way around." I noticed the older man's color had improved; there was a heightened sense of purpose in his posture and attitude. I suspected the tensions of the past few hours had gotten his adrenalin flowing, an antidote to the sadness and grief he displayed when we first met him.

"On the contrary, Joan Elizabeth, the scheme was yours. I remember as a child it was you who always led in the make-believe games you and your sister Sarah played. An imaginative, inventive child, I told my wife Helene."

I smiled at his compliment. At the time I thought we were simply nuisances to the French couple, beyond their notice or caring.

Dan returned in a few minutes, shaking his head. "No dice, Cupcake. Not an ambulance to be had, for love nor money. They were all commandeered for the army. We have a station wagon Major Everett reluctantly said we could use, but we'll have to rewrite the scenario. The professor will have to drive and answer questions, I'll be the doctor, you can be the patient. Or do you want to toss a coin for the supporting roles?"

He waited for my decision. "I'll be the nurse, Dan. You can be doubled up in agony so you won't have to explain anything to anyone. The professor can talk for both of us, I'm sure."

"Shucks, I thought we'd have a chance to play doctor. Haven't done that since I was ten," Dan teased.

I hadn't heard quite the same phraseology in England but knew full well what he meant. I confronted him with as much dignity as I could muster. "This isn't a game, Daniel. Try to be serious."

"What makes you think I'm not?"

I rolled my eyes at his impertinence. He responded with an unrepentant grin.

We all turned as Major Everett entered the room, car keys in hand. "Whoever the patient is going to be won't be very comfortable," he advised us. "I found a quilt you can use as a mattress and the nurse in the infirmary got together a medical kit in an overnight bag for you, but you're going to have to ad-lib if you're stopped. By the way, who is the patient? I have to know if the French authorities call here to check."

"Me, sir," Dan announced. "Miss Poynton will be the nurse, Professor Aubuchon the driver." He turned to the professor to ask, "You can drive, can't you, sir?"

The scientist nodded. "What will I be driving?"

"Chrysler Town and Country station wagon, three-speed transmission."

"I can manage."

The obliging nurse had also furnished a uniform which I donned over my skirt and blouse, necessary because it was several sizes too large for me. No disguise was needed for Dan or the professor. The former climbed into the back of the wagon lying on the poorly cushioned floor, the professor in the driver's seat depressed the clutch, familiarizing himself with the gears. I scrambled in back with Dan clutching my nurse's kit, sitting by his side, finding it impossible to get comfortable until I sat cross-legged, hoping my skirt was long enough for modesty. Dan was gentlemanly, staring resolutely up at the dome-light. Evidently he was getting into the mood. I heard a couple of piteous groans and bit my lip, trying not to smile. "Great performance," I assured him.

"Performance nothing," he complained. "You try lying on this damn platform, Cupcake. I'm going to have a broken back by the time we get to wherever we're going."

Chapter Five

Dan and I both shuddered as we started out the embassy gate, the noise of the gears grinding as the professor shifted made us uneasy. Out of the corner of my eye I saw Major Everett wince. The guard opened the gate, we drove out slowly, and soon the professor got the feel of the transmission.

Dan reached for my hand and held it as we proceeded out of town. I raised my eyebrows as he explained, "I'm in so much pain I need to be comforted." The man was irrepressible, but I admitted to myself the physical contact helped to sooth the tension I was feeling. Could we get away with this hastily concocted scheme? The professor swerved to avoid a pile of miscellaneous belongings in the middle of the road. A handcart with a broken wheel sat by the curb and I pitied the family or person who was forced to abandon precious possessions. The sudden maneuver made me lose balance; I began to tip toward the patient.

I felt Dan's arms holding me, to keep me from falling, then, to my surprise, he pulled me down to his chest where I sprawled awkwardly. His lips against mine were the next thing I felt as he kissed me thoroughly, fervently. I provided no resistance to his advances. This kiss was not the same as we had pantomimed on the road earlier on the way to the professor. It was controlled, then, as I found myself responding, more insistent, demanding. When I tried to pull away, shaken with my emotions, Dan held me tightly, parting my lips slightly with his tongue. I tried to pull back then found myself eagerly seeking his mouth again.

His eyes were open, watching me as I parted my lips again, touching his tongue lightly with mine, aware I was shivering. I had had young men kiss me before, but never experienced the sophisticated technique of this American. I tried to ignore the restless upsurge of feeling I was experiencing, not ready to label it desire, but well aware of its compelling nature. "We haven't got time for this now," I remonstrated as I broke away from his embrace, wondering on how many other girls he had employed the same knowing, seductive technique.

He nodded. "You're right. But it felt good, didn't it?" Against my will I nodded.

"Pay attention," the Professor said softly "Another barricade coming up."

Although we had no rehearsal, the gendarmes believed the emergency we were dealing with was genuine. One of them directed us to the tuberculosis clinic and wished us luck. He said he had heard the patients and staff had been evacuated the day before. The professor thanked him in a rough, working-man's patois and drove away, this time managing the shift with no difficulty.

We jounced along in the vehicle, over a dirt road that became narrower and more difficult to traverse. I tried to read the hand-drawn map with the aid of the domelight and hoped I was not misleading the Professor. The road was empty ahead of us, hedgerows on each side, seemingly guarding our passageway. I wondered if anyone lived nearby. The isolation gave us a sense of safety, that surely no patrols would be out at that hour.

It was past ten o'clock and I was becoming more anxious. If it turned out we were lost, we would have precious little time to reverse course and find another direction.

"How's the gas gauge?" Dan asked from his prone position. I leaned over the passenger seat and squinted at the dashboard. "Still three-quarters of a tank," I reported.

I was too optimistic. Suddenly up ahead we saw an army truck and three soldiers, rifles extended, flagging us down. The Professor stopped and rapidly (too rapidly for me to fully understand) explained what the problem was, that he was transporting a critically ill man to the Sisters of Mercy. Could they please tell him if he was headed in the right direction? A two-minute conference—then one of the soldiers climbed in through the tailgate and looked at the patient who, on cue, emitted low, agonized groans. In my less-than-perfect French I explained I was the patient's nurse, a cousin from England, and that I was afraid if we didn't get him to medical help immediately the appendix might rupture.

He gestured for me to lower Dan's trousers and show him where it hurt. Expressionless, I hoped, I unloosened the belt buckle, unbuttoned the fly and drew the pants aside, gently touching the right-hand side of Dan's abdomen. A groan. Gritting of teeth. Clenching of fist. I tried not to look at the triangle of dark hair traveling from his navel downward, or admit to myself that I even noticed it.

Evidently Dan's stellar performance was convincing. The quick motion upward with his hand told me I could cover the patient up. Dan cooperated, turning on his side with great difficulty, drawing his knees upward and moaning softly. I laid my hand on his forehead and shook my head with a worried expression on my face, hoping the soldier would assume I meant the patient was feverish.

The three soldiers conferred then finally the leader nodded and told the Professor we could go on. The small hospital would be on our right, beyond a closely massed group of Lombardy poplars. He wished us luck and hit the rear left fender to indicate we could proceed.

I waited for some sort of comment from Dan as he fastened his trousers and was grateful none was forthcoming. All he said was, "You managed that just fine, Cupcake."

"Your performance would have convinced any Hartley Street specialist you were on the verge of expiring," I complimented him. He frowned, then realized I referred to the street where many of London's outstanding physicians practised.

In spite of my wariness I realized I was becoming more and more attracted to this young American, good intentions notwithstanding. He was resourceful, willing to adjust to the needs of the occasion and, much to my surprise, quick to adapt to my position as leader of the operation. Despite our kisses, which I chalked up to opportunity, he had refrained from embarrassing me over the exposure of his body. I watched his contortions as he attempted to find a comfortable position. He was reluctant to sit up. In the event we were stopped again he might not have time to lie back and go into his suffering patient mode. The lower portion of my anatomy was growing numb from its constant impact against the floor of the station wagon and I was certain he was suffering to a greater degree than me.

I heard him ask in a low voice, "Cupcake, when we accomplish this mission how am I going to get in touch with you? Will you give me your address in England?"

As much as I wanted to accede to his request, I had to think about it. It would not be a good idea to have it circulating about in the event we were picked up and detained and I was not sure if it would be allowed by my superior. I finally said, "You could have Major Everett contact General Hartley and see if he will provide it. I don't know what else to tell you. How about you? Could I reach you in the States or in England?"

"Box 666, New York 17, New York. It's an accommodation address, but I can be reached there." He took my hand, pressed it to his lips, eyes searching mine and said, "I don't want this to end here, Joan. Somehow we have to get together, later, or when this whole mess is settled." Neither of us knew we were speaking in terms of five year's hence.

His eyes were focused on mine, reading my thoughts I believed. He reached up to draw me down to him again, his hands sliding along the sides of my breasts, but he made no attempt to fondle me when he felt me stiffen at his touch. The Professor, who was probably glancing in the rear-view mirror, cleared his throat loudly. "Joan Elizabeth, you will have to keep watch on the right for me. I can just about manage to steer in the ruts, let alone search for the hospital." There was a gentle reproof in his voice which we both deserved. It was no time for romantic dalliance, no matter how much we both wanted it. Dan held my hand tightly and looked up at the car's ceiling, his respiration as rapid as mine. Where will we go from here, I wondered. I realized there was no turning back, at least for me.

What had begun as a flirtation now had assumed for me a much, much deeper meaning.

Three-quarters of an hour later I spied the low stone fence and sign which identified the sanitarium.

"Okay, that's the hospital we're supposed to be going to, Joan. Now what?"

"We drive on for another two, two-and-a-half miles to a crossroads, take a left and try to see the monastery on the right. It's so dark now I'm afraid we might miss it although there is starlight." A full moon would have made it easier for us and the airplane we were hoped to meet. It would also make us a thousand times more visible to any enemy soldiers who might be in advance of the main Nazi invasion.

Our luck held. We were probably becoming used to the dark, but it was Dan, reclining on one elbow, who spotted the silhouette of the ruined monastery rising over fields of rubble. No attempt had been made to plow the fields in preparation for winter; perhaps the farmers were conscripted or realized there was no reason to make an effort to provide crops for their enemy, or fodder for animals, since everything would be commandeered for German use. My eyes strained to find an opening which would accommodate the big American station wagon and finally saw a break in the hedgerows, probably intended for the farmer's horse and plow.

"Drive through the opening quickly, then cut the lights," Dan ordered the Professor. "It's so dark car lights in a suspicious place will bring troops at once." Professor Aubuchon quickly complied. We bumped jarringly across the fields toward the monastery when the outline of men's figures appeared suddenly before us. "What the hell—" Dan swore as we slowed down, stopped, and waited to see what would happen next.

I could hear a few French phrases, the Professor replied, turned to us and said, "It's all right. They're patriots. They've had a message from General Barclay—" he looked at me quickly to see if the name was significant. I nodded. "We are to abandon this vehicle and proceed to the monastery. They will take us the rest of the way to the landing strip in a farm wagon. Somehow the Germans saw us leave the embassy in the station wagon and have been in touch with a platoon nearby. Make haste, you two. We have only minutes to spare."

I groped for my briefcase and purse, turned to Dan to ask, "Can you find your way back from here?" I handed him the map, although I would have preferred to retain it myself.

He shook his head. "I'm going with you, at least to the landing field. I have to make certain you and the professor get off the ground. I can find my way back to the car tomorrow morning if I have to and drive it back to the Embassy." My heart sank. We had, at best, maybe three more hours together.

I nodded. "All right," turning away so he wouldn't see the glint of tears in my eyes.

"We have to go now, Joan Elizabeth," Professor Aubuchon stated. "The wagon is over there by the side of the building."

Chapter Six

The patriots told us, in broken English, that we were all to lie down, close to each other, in the center of the wagon while they piled hay over us. The narrow slats of the wagon sides were pulled up and we were told not to say a word when we reached the dirt road again. The scent of the hay was fragrant, but I hoped no one of us would sneeze. Our nostrils were full of dust and bits of fragrant dried grasses. I lay in the middle between both men and before we started Dan carefully turned me toward him, drawing me against his body protectively but, of course, his close presence was seductive in itself and I trembled slightly as his arms encircled me. How could I bear to be separated from him before daylight? I was sure he could feel my heart pounding against his chest as he held me close. I inhaled his male scent and buried my face against his shirt front, the tension we were under intensifying what I realized was my heightened response to his warm, close body. I knew I had to gain control over my thoughts and concentrate on our surroundings and the possibility of imminent danger and discovery. We were not the only lovers who were spending our last minutes together and I was honor-bound to carry out my mission, not lose myself in emotion.

The horse pulled the wagon slowly along, swaying, our bodies jouncing back and forth. The professor had elected tactfully to lay with his back toward us. Dan and I pressed close together, not daring to let our hands explore, our lips touch in a kiss. We had to be content with proximity only. I felt Dan's breath stir my hair slightly and I carefully, ever so slowly positioned my head to lay tucked in against his shoulder. I was puzzled when Dan whispered, "This is some hayride!" then I recalled reading about young people in a story riding in such manner to a square dance. Or church social. Quilting bee? Harvest supper? Whatever they did in America. As I recalled, they rode on top of the hay, not huddled together, bodies tantalized by every bump and jolt in the road.

34

In spite of our intense awareness of one another, the strain of the evening's events, the unspoken fear we would be accosted and arrested, the lateness of the hour made us both sleepy. We relaxed, dozing, lulled by the rhythm of the horse's gait, trying to be content with the nearness of each other. I could hear the late spring sounds around us, the clacking sound of some kind of frog, the rustle of birds' wings as they fluttered in a tree overhanging the road, repositioning themselves on a branch and, in the distance, the sharp bark of a dog alert to some presence around him. I lived in the country in England and the sounds made me homesick for the safety and security of the familiar.

It was too good to last. Ahead were voices, a light which penetrated the layers of straw and more voices speaking French. What now, I thought. Had our luck run out? But if it were the enemy they would surely have been speaking in German.

I heard Professor Aubuchon replying to one particularly deep voice, then the name of General Barclay distinctly reached my ears. The Professor's soft "Oui," agreed with the Frenchman's statement and the next thing I knew the hay was being carefully removed from all of us. I was puzzled as to how Deep Voice knew Aubuchon was with until I heard the Professor say, "Joan Elizabeth, I know this man. I have spoken to him before. He tells us we are transfer to his car and be taxied to the landing strip. Do you wish to question this change in plans?"

"Would you ask him by whose authority the change has been made?" I already suspected it was General Barclay's which was immediately confirmed by Deep Voice stating the General's first and last name.

"He wants to know which one of you is in charge of this exercize."

I stepped forward, gave him my name and whispered certain words in Deep Voice's ear. I waited for his response nervously, but the reply was as I had been told to expect. "Your name?" I asked as he looked askance at what I am sure he believed to be too young a woman to be in authority. I stood quietly trying to project as confident an image as possible waiting for his reply.

He told me simply his name was Pierre, that no last name was necessary, and that he had been told he would be meeting a young woman and an older gentlemen. Who, he asked, indicating Dan, was this young man? My fiance? He had not been told to expect anyone else. I told Dan to show him his credentials from the American embassy. Pierre, looking even more dubious, read them twice, shrugged, returning them with the comment, "You may as well come to the landing strip so you can satisfy your superiors all went as planned." Dan nodded and made no reply. I knew the fact of our youth bothered Pierre who appeared to be in his middle to late thirties.

Once again we transferred to another vehicle, I making certain my briefcase and purse were with me. Our driver was in his late twenties, handsome, fair-haired, with a charming smile to go with his French accent. He spoke English, but it was not grammatical. However, we able to get the gist of his words, that he had just arrived lately to the area and only Pierre knew of him. His home was close to the Swiss border.

Dan was American, was he not? He could tell I was Anglais. Too bad we were in France under such alarming circumstances. Perhaps we could return at some other time and enjoy the charms of his country. He explained in his halting English that he had been a taxi driver in Paris and would be more than happy to provide a tour of la belle Paris. I smiled and told him we would be enchanted to, but now we had to make haste and get to the landing strip to meet our rendezvous with the small plane. At that he turned on his engine and we were off, once again bumping along the rutted dirt road. The Professor sat in front and Dan and I listened carefully to their conversation, most of which we had difficulty in understanding. Dan whispered in my ear, "Do you know what they're saying?"

I shook my head. "No, they're talking too fast." He nodded in agreement.

The Professor turned around to face us at that point and told us the driver heard there was another roadblock up ahead, just before our turnoff to the landing strip. "German or French?" I asked. No one knew. I was beginning to worry. We had less than three-quarters of an hour to get there and I knew the pilot would not wait longer than five minutes, if that, for us. I was also worried about Dan's safety. Would he be able to get back to the American embassy? In fact, would the embassy be there when he got back? I had noticed boxes piled in the corners of the hallways, a sure sign that evacuation was imminent.

At that point the driver swung the car off onto a side path. I glanced behind us to see what looked like a transport truck crossing the road with lights dimmed. Was that part of the roadblock? We watched for a few minutes to see if more trucks would appear, then decided to take our chances back on the primary road. By some miracle the driver was able to back up the twenty-five feet or so without hitting anything. The road was so narrow he could never have turned the car around. Once we were headed in the right direction, the driver told us it would be only fifteen or so minutes to our destination.

Fifteen minutes! Only a quarter of an hour remained for Dan and I to be together. I sighed and turned to him, to feel his arms come quickly around me, holding me tightly. I felt his lips brush my hair, then cross my cheek to my mouth. He kissed me lightly then suddenly with bruising intensity. I heard him murmur, "I promise I'll find you somehow, Joan."

"No promises, Dan." I replied. "If it happens, it happens. We may never see each other again and—"I couldn't finish, but I wanted him to know how much I cared. "It's been a lifetime in less than twenty-four hours. I'll never forget you, never." I slipped my arms underneath his jacket, holding him tightly, trembling as I felt the heat of his body as he returned my embrace.

Chapter Seven

Lights ahead. Trucks across the road. Soldiers standing at attention. Maybe we would be spending a great deal of time together, in prison. The driver braked, turning quickly to face us saying "Let me talk," and got out of the car. He took the leader to one side and spoke quietly to him. By this time we had determined the men were French and, if not friendly, not about to detain us, I hoped. Once I heard a couple of guttural German phrases and looked at Dan in dismay, but knew there was nothing we could do. The driver had taken the keys with him, for our safety I hoped, so that the truck could not be taken, but we couldn't get away either, if the need arose.

The two men came back to us, the one following the driver shining a flashlight on the ground so that the driver could see his way. As they neared us, the torch-bearer stumbled and light shone full on the driver's handsome, smiling face, revealing a scar across one cheek. It resembled a dueling scar, but he was French, wasn't he?

He got into the front seat and turned to us and announced, "It's just a—how you say?—technical thing. We are to follow him. He will guide us to our destination. About ten minutes more, we are there."

Follow him meant just what he said. The torch-bearer walked as swiftly as possible in front of the car while I fretted., "We'll never get there on time." I heard Dan fumbling around but it was too dark to see what he was doing. He seemed to be scratching his leg, or so I guessed as the cuff of his trousers brushed my ankle. Perhaps chaff from the hay remained and was annoying him.

The lane, for it was no more than that, veered to the left, curving around an ancient tree. The torch-bearer disappeared from sight. We had not been using headlights but parking lights which were partially obscured by paint, except for a slit which permitted dim illumination of the terrain directly in front of us.

Just before the driver extinguished the light I could see what appeared to be a clearing ahead of us and hoped that we had reached the site of the landing field.

Suddenly the passenger-side front door was pulled open. Two men reached inside, grabbed the professor and pulled him out of the car. I know I screamed "Stop!" as Dan leaned forward to press a pistol against the back of the driver's head.

"Tell them to get that man back in the car or I'll shoot," Dan threatened, but the driver shrugged.

"Look around you. You'll be dead in seconds."

He was right. The ancient taxi was surrounded on both sides by more men, men in French uniforms, but I realized they were probably German soldiers in disguise. The Professor was already lost to sight.

I head Dan cock the pistol. "Okay, then, floor the accelerator and drive to that field ahead as fast as you can. I don't give a damn if you hit someone. Get us out of here, pronto." He shoved the gun against the side of the man's throat, under his ear, leaving no doubt to his intent. The driver released the clutch, floored the accelerator and the car rumbled and bounced across the field.

"What about Professor Aubuchon?" I screamed at Dan. "We have to bring him with us!" I was frantic, knowing we had been bested at the last minute.

"You have his papers; they'll have to do. There's no way we can get him back—we're outnumbered. Better if I can get you to the plane—at least your superiors will have some of the information they need. Look ahead!" Across the field I could see headlights spaced evenly along the field, lighting the way for the expected plane to land. I heard the sound of the approaching engine, close overhead.

Dan pressed the gun harder against the driver's neck. "Drive fast until I tell you to stop. Pull in to the right of the last vehicle along the runway. Do it now!"

We swerved into line, Dan yelled, "Get out now, Joan," and as I scrambled out of the car I saw Dan's arm swing in an arc and hit the driver with the butt end of the gun on his temple. Leaping out of the car after me, he grabbed my arm, still holding the briefcase and my purse, and ran with me to the plane which had just touched down. We could see the pilot gesturing for us to hurry and get aboard and I turned to Dan, "Come with me, Dan. There's room—you'll never get back by yourself. They'll capture you. We can have British Intelligence clear it with your embassy." God, how I wanted him safe on that plane with me!

He hesitated, shook his head. "Those weren't my orders. I was only to get you and the Professor to the rendezvous."

We heard the sound of rifle fire coming towards us through the woods. I shook my head. "Don't argue. Get on board! We'll all be captured and shot." He knew I was right and pushed me toward the door, helping me to climb on board.

I heard a British voice asking, "Is this your cargo, Miss Poynton?" indicating Dan.

"No, the Professor's been taken captive. This man has to come with me. He's attached to the American embassy."

The pilot realized there was no time for arguing, gunning his engine as we spoke. Three men were advancing across the field at a run. We pulled the airplane door shut, fastened our seat belts, instinctively ducking down in our seats as a shower of bullets traced our pathway down the field, one or two penetrating the sides of the airplane. I heard the pilot mutter, "Don't hit the gas tanks!" and then we were airborne. The actual time involved could not have been more than two or three minutes but it had that eerie quality of slow-motion film as we left the ground, barely clearing the trees at the end of the field.

Once safely aloft I experienced that let-down feeling after extreme exertion and physical fear. I touched my waist to make certain the oilskin pouch was still fastened around my body, but knew the Professor himself was needed to interpret and explain the meaning of his experimental data. I was too young, too inexperienced. British Intelligence should never have entrusted such an important mission to me. Weeping, I turned to Dan and through my tears lamented the fact we had failed.

"You did your best, Joan," Dan tried to comfort me. "You had no way of predicting betrayal at the end. We both thought the driver and Pierre were legitimate, even the Professor. We were lucky to get out alive."

"It wasn't luck. It was you. I didn't know you had a gun. You and I would have been killed after they took the professor. I realize that now."

I thought of Professor Aubuchon in the hands of the Germans and wondered what his fate would be. Would they kill him after they extracted the information they needed? I thought not. Somehow he would be kept alive and made to contribute his knowledge to their efforts. But my thoughts were with the lonely old man who had lost his wife and I regretted the fact he had also lost his chance for freedom.

I reached across the narrow aisle to touch Dan's face, wanting to be closer to him but afraid to ignore the pilot's instructions we were to stay belted at all times. I was startled when I felt warm liquid on my fingers. Blood, I suddenly realized. "Dan, you've been hurt. How—"

"I think a bullet grazed me. It's okay, I'll live. It stings, but it's nothing worse."

I handed him a handkerchief and told him to press on the surface wound to stop the bleeding, hoping it was no more serious than he told me.

The pilot's course took us directly over the English Channel. Below I could see a steady stream of small boats approaching the French shore and asked the pilot what they were doing.

"The British Expeditionary Force is huddled on the beach at Dunkirk awaiting transport—those are British fishing boats and private cruisers—anything with a motor."

Later, much later, I realized I was eyewitness to one of the most stirring and patriotic events of the war, the efforts of my countrymen to rescue our remaining troops in France. I felt tears on my face as I realized the enormity of the undertaking. There were those brave men and here was I who had utterly failed in my mission.

Dan saw my tears and tried to reassure me over the roar of the engines. "Joan, you did your best. Don't agonize over it. What choice did you have at the end?"

I knew we had none. His level-headed analysis helped sooth my terrible feelings of guilt and inadequacy. I had tried to do my best and if it hadn't been for Dan, would not have been able to get to the plane. I regretted the fact he had been injured in trying to help me through his government's orders to involve himself in my crusade. Again, nervously, I touched my waist to reassure myself the oilskin pouch was securely in place.

"Put your head back and relax, at least until we approach our landing site," the pilot suggested, and wearily I did so. I glanced again at Dan and in the dim light I saw lines of fatigue and a drained, drawn look on his face. He hadn't lost that much blood I thought, but was suffering from the same degree of tension and nerve strain as me.

As we flew on we could see below us a steady stream of the same small craft we had spotted at the beginning of the flight. This time it was a group returning from Dunkirk to England, fishing boats this time, I thought, with a British destroyer herding them along.

We landed just as the slightest streak of light appeared behind us in the east. I thanked the pilot then turned to search for any transport that might be provided for us. I didn't recognize where we landed and knew I would have extreme difficulty finding my way back to headquarters in London, if I could by some miracle find a car and sufficient petrol to get us there. Dan was standing by my side, slightly unsteady, even though he had his arm around my shoulder to support me. We were both absolutely exhausted.

I was still looking around, trying to decide what to do next when I saw a car with dimmed parking lights approach us on the tarmac, drawing up to park close by. General Barclay alighted and my heart fell at the thought of having to recount our failure.

He listened in silence, his face grave. As I began to apologize for my inability to complete the mission he shook his head. "You're not to blame, Miss Poynton. Somewhere, somehow there was a weak link in our lines of communication. Our support system was hastily assembled and it was only at the last minute we decided to resort to the US Embassy for assistance." His eyes shifted to Dan. "Thank you for all you did, Mr. Childress. I have sealed orders for you back in my office, but I doubt very much we can return you to the Paris embassy. At this point, I'm not certain there is an American Embassy in Paris. I'll have to ask you both to come with me for a debriefing, then we'll try and arrange accommodations for you both."

"I have the use of my aunt's apartment in London," I interposed. "It would be only Mr. Childress who would need housing."

The General nodded. "We'll tend to that directly."

Irrepressibly, Dan murmured in my ear. "How about a boarder? I can cook."

One glance reassured me that meal preparation was not the service he had in mind. I shook my head, smiling, hoping the General had not overheard our quick interchange.

We sat in the rear seat of the car, occasionally drifting off into fitful slumber as the car proceeded to London in the misty, early-morning light, our hands clasped as we rode. I hoped the General would not notice. After a brief interview, during which time I turned over the oilskin pouch and its contents which were whisked off to some other section of the building, we both described in as much detail as possible the events of the past night. We were able to describe Pierre quite accurately, and I did my best to recall to mind the traitorous driver's appearance. I mentioned the scar on his face, his manner of speaking and his easy manner which had inspired our confidence. The General made no comment but asked his secretary through the intercom to bring in a file under the name "Dieter."

Opening it, he asked us to confirm a few more questions then, sighing, said, "Dieter is probably our man. He's a well-known French collaborator—his mother was French, his father

Prussian. He's full of charm with an aptitude for inspiring confidence. Slippery as the devil. If we ever catch up with him after the war, his number's up."

After the war seemed an impossible concept to grasp just then.

It was obvious to General Barclay we were exhausted. He rose and gestured toward the door. "Off you two go. If you aren't too tired, we can meet again for dinner and talk some more. I'll give you a call late this afternoon, Miss Poynton, and we can make arrangements." He then shook Dan's hand. "Mr. Childress, thank you again and I will ask you to call Miss Poynton about five o'clock to confirm our arrangements." He courteously walked us to the door, delaying Dan's departure by telling him he wanted someone to check the abrasion on his face from the bullet.

Dan and I looked at each other, both of us wanting very much to embrace, a fact that seemed immediately apparent to the general who discreetly turned back into his office. A quick hug and a peck on the cheek had to suffice, then Dan said softly, "I'll see you tonight, Cupcake. Get some sleep while you can."

Chapter Eight

My Aunt Sylvia had a bed-sitter in Belgravia. I wearily opened the door with the key I had carried with me in my purse, put all my possessions on the floor by the bed, pulled back the covers and wearily sank back onto the mattress. We had a light breakfast in General Barclay's office and I was too tired to think about fixing something else. I saw Dan's face in my mind, grateful that we would have a few hours together before whatever might be my next assignment, or his return to duty. It was my last thought before I sank into oblivion.

I awoke about three o'clock that afternoon, still tired, but knowing I would get no more sleep at that point. I opened the hot water spigot in the bathtub, wondering if there would be means to take a bath at that hour of the day, and found slightly more than tepid water running. I said goodbye to the luxurious soaking I had planned, climbed in, washed, shampooed and rinsed my hair in what was now cold running water. Aunt Sylvia's towels were soft, prewar, thick turkish toweling and I dried swiftly, uncomfortable in the cold air that chilled my damp body. Fortunately, my hair was naturally curly, so all it required was a quick rub with the towel and a flick of the comb to make it presentable.

I had been too tired to rinse out any underwear and my stockings were in shreds, but I ruthlessly searched through my aunt's gossamer-thin silk French lingerie for something fresh to wear. I had given her a half-dozen pairs of silk stockings for Christmas a year ago and prayed that at least one pair could be found. I craned my head to check the straightness of the seams on my legs and then walked across the room to the big wardrobe in search of a dress I knew I had left behind on my last visit to London. The dark green suited my fair skin and hair and I shamelessly appropriated a triple strand of pearls and gold earrings to complete the costume. I looked in the triple mirror at the dressing table and hoped Dan would approve of the young woman I saw reflected, in spite of the dark shadows under my eyes. I hesitated, then added a touch of rouge to complement my lipstick.

The general's voice greeted me as I sprang to answer the phone, suggesting that I tell Mr. Childress to escort me to a very elegant restaurant in the West End. We were to be seated under his reservation until he arrived, which he thought would be around six o'clock. "If I'm not there by then," he instructed me, "you both go ahead and order. Something may come up at the last minute. The bill will go on my account; don't you concern yourself with it." He hesitated then added, "Joan, I'm very proud of you. Your bravery is to be commended." Rarely did the General who was a close family friend through the years treat me any differently from those under his command. I was pleased that he had made an exception under the present circumstances. I thanked him and hung up, calling Dan next to tell him of the evening's agenda. He told me to expect him shortly.

He had evidently taken advantage of the valet service at the hotel, for he arrived in freshly pressed suit and newly laundered shirt. As he helped me on with my raincoat he whistled and told me, "You look smashing, Miss Poynton. Isn't that the proper English term?" I laughed and said yes, adding he looked pretty smashing, too.

"We colonials don't want to put ourselves to shame," he replied. I realized in a fraction of a second he was referring to the United States Revolutionary War by that term.

The restaurant was nearly empty at that early hour. The General's name worked magic. The drinks were superb, the appetizers delicious, the entree above reproach. We knew it was highly unlikely that General Barclay would be free to join us; he had simply provided us with time to be together, alone. We ended the meal with coffee, which surprised Dan. "I thought all you English drank tea," he commented, but I told him no, not usually after dinner. At least my family didn't. We lingered over coffee and brandy and then I asked him, "What did your embassy say? Can you tell me?"

"No problem," he assured me. "But—" he hesitated for a second. "I have to fly back to the States tomorrow afternoon, if I can be gotten on the flight to Lisbon." He looked me full in the eye "This will be our last night together."

I had hoped against hope we would have a few days before we had to part. I had anticipated perhaps a forty-eight to seventy-two hour debriefing and kept my fingers crossed Dan wouldn't be needed during that time. I knew I had to make a very swift decision about the remainder of our time together. I met his gaze, not knowing how to proceed, not wanting to assume things that might not be an option on his part. We were silent for a moment, then Dan asked softly, "Will you come back to the hotel with me tonight?" I could see the look of apprehension on his face, for all his flirtatiousness and Yankee bravado. I suppose every man is terrified at the thought of rejection.

I hesitated. It wasn't a matter of conviction or morals or religion. I knew I would say yes, longed to say yes, even before asked, but I wanted him to know it wasn't a casual thing for me. It wasn't a conquest. It was a choice I would make because I loved him. Even if we never saw each other again, I knew I would be poorer all my life if I passed up this chance to be with him.

I nodded and put my hand on his. "Dan, you must know I'm not saying yes lightly. This has to mean something to both of us. Do you understand?" My eyes pleaded for assurance that he honoured my statement.

He answered quietly, "I understand, Joan. It may be only this one night that we can be together, but it's something we both have to have, to do. I love you, Joan Poynton. I'd ask you to marry me, but there's no time, no time at all. I don't expect promises that we may never be able to keep, but I think we both want this night to remember."

I thought how trite the most profound statements could sound, even when they were the honest outpouring of our thoughts and emotions. I gathered my purse, my aunt's gloves, and we proceeded to look for a taxi. As we stood at the curb I thought his hotel would be so impersonal, the site of so many assignations, not truly where I wanted to be with him. "Let's go to my place, Dan. My aunt is away and we can be more comfortable." As if comfort was our primary concern.

"Fine," he said briefly. I knew he was as tense as I, ridden with longing and desire.

Would I know how what to do, how to please him? I was apprehensive although I wanted with all my heart for him to take me. His touch set me afire and for all we knew we would never have this chance again. Once inside the taxi he reached for me and what began as a gentle, reassuring kiss soon became a searching, demanding passionate seeking for one another. His hands slipped beneath my raincoat seeking my breasts and I arched eagerly against the tantalizing slow stroke of his fingers.

As I look back now I wonder how we could have been so thoughtless, so single-minded in gratifying our passion that we never gave a thought to preventing conception. It was no more Dan's fault than mine. We simply ignored the possibility. We were young, the terrible urgency of wartime and the driving, overwhelming urge to couple overcame any rational thought. Even now, despite all the events that followed, I smile at our innocence and regret not for one minute the child we conceived that night.

We awoke tangled in each other's arms the next morning. I felt like Scarlett O'Hara the night after Rhett Butler carried her up that dark staircase—even better, for all I knew. Beside me Dan stirred, opened sleepy eyes and reached over to kiss me as thoroughly and intensely as the night before. I nodded yes to his unspoken question and once again we made eager yet bittersweet love, knowing we had only a few hours left to be together.

Chapter Nine

Later that afternoon I stood on the tarmac as Dan climbed aboard the plane that would carry him to Lisbon where he would connect with another flight to the United States. He turned, our eyes caught for one brief second, I waved as he gazed at me and then, at the stewardess's request, he turned to enter the plane. I was too far away to see him, even if he sat at a window facing me. I watched the plane taxi down the runway, come airborne, and then diminish in size as it circled around to set its course. I saw a squadron of RAF fighter planes in the distance and prayed that any air combat would be far from the plane carrying my love.

I hadn't told Dan, but I was due back at headquarters late that afternoon to discuss a future assignment. I sat waiting for General Barclay to finish his conference call, near tears, but attempting to gain composure as I forced myself to dwell on the present. That evening, I promised myself, I would recall in detail and longing the hours Dan and I had spent together.

"You'll be flown back to the same airstrip where we picked you up two nights ago," I heard the general saying. "There you will be met and given the details of your mission." I had heard the barest outline only a few minutes ago and I was aghast. I was to be taken as a prisoner to the same camp where Professor Aubuchon was being held, make contact with him, and through as-yet unspecified arrangements bring him out to meet Pierre who would make certain we had the means to reach England. The thought of a Nazi prison camp terrified me and it must have shown on my face because General Barclay tried to reassure me. "I guarantee you, you'll be brought back safely, Joan. I realize you've been through a bad time these past few weeks but again, you are the only one who can identify the professor. We must have him if we are to interpret the notes you brought to us. It is absolutely essential that we do so. We believe it will shorten the

49

war by weeks, if not months. You have no option. You *must* go."

I knew he was right. I knew my duty and I knew I alone could convince the professor to escape with me. Even if at that point I had known I had conceived a child, I would have had to go anyway. There was no way to refuse. My life and my child's life were of no import balanced against Britain's need for the Professor's knowledge.

Afterwards I vowed I would try to forget the horror of the camp and the abject terror the professor and I experienced during our escape. Until I told Dan at a later time of the events, I had believed I had pretty well submerged the details in my subconsciousness. The worst thing, as I found out a month later, was the fact that I was pregnant and dreaded the thought I might lose Dan's baby from the lack of proper food, the threat of dysentery and the unbelievable stresses we endured in our journey back to France, then England. I had lost two stone weight and was exhausted, mentally, physically and spiritually.

I was taken by ambulance directly to hospital from the plane, running a fever and too weak to lift my head. The General was shocked at my appearance and the next day apologized for my ordeal. "Your father would never forgive me, Joan, if he knew what I had asked you to do," he stated in a rare display of remorse.

I hesitated, then told him outright I was pregnant and would have to resign from His Majesty's service. I wanted to take no chances on losing my child. Would he please, I asked, find the means to contact Dan so I could tell him about our child? I wondered if we could not be married by proxy.

I should have realized when General Barclay, who had been listening to me with a grave expression on his face, reached over and took my hand, clearing his throat. I thought I was going to get a lecture on morals from my father's old friend and how I had let down the service and was mentally bracing myself for his condemnation. Instead, he told me that Dan's plane had been shot down by the Luftwaffe as it passed over the bottom of

England on its way to Lisbon. There were no survivors, nor traces of debris from the plane scattered over the ocean's surface. "I'm sorry, Joan, to be the one to tell you of this sad event. At least you had—" he fumbled for words, "—a few brief hours together." He sought my eye and added, "Should you change your mind about the baby, perhaps we could make other arrangements—" his voice ending on a tentative note.

He hadn't finished the sentence when I whispered, "No, never. I want my child." He nodded acceptance of my statement. I turned away, knowing there was nothing more to be said and heard him softly close the door behind him as he departed.

I was tearless as I faced the window, unable to comprehend what he had told me. I had heard the words but could not accept them as fact. It was then John entered the room and I saw him for the first time, hypodermic in hand. I was scarcely aware of the passage of the needle into my upper arm. He murmured, "This will relax you, Miss Poynton. General Barclay told me you had just received bad news."

I nodded and within a minute or so lapsed into a drug-induced sleep.

It was John Ferguson who was my primary physician. He saw me several times a day as I slowly recovered strength and appetite, examined me and assured me my baby was all right, and when I felt able to talk listened intently without comment while I explained about Dan and I. He had a sympathetic, half-smile on his face, but I sensed no condemnation, no attempt to make me feel guilty. His expression was kindness and compassion itself.

John had an interesting face. Not handsome; fine- featured, a sensitive mouth and warm, caring eyes. He listened carefully and with complete attention to my story. As I finished my tale he told me quietly, "I imagine that night was magical for both of you. These are unusual times and you must never blame yourself, Miss Poynton. As a man I would have wanted you very much and you were right in accepting him. It was an act of generosity and love and I commend you for your actions."

What an extraordinary man, I thought. Most of the time I felt like worn goods and imagined no man would realize what I did was for love, not lust or passion. John patted my hand and told me he would see me the next morning. I cried myself to sleep as always, but somehow I felt my spirits lighten as I thought about John's understanding and consoling words. Instead of quiet acceptance I expected that perhaps he might offer the means for an abortion, either performed by himself or someone else. I never, never would have allowed it. I welcomed John's visits as a physician and at the end of his tour of duty when he would often stop by just to chat. We shared a mutual love of literature and I found him bright and incisive in his comments. Our visits were brief, but I looked forward always to seeing him.

I rested, ate well, read books John had lent me and more quickly than I imagined possible, regained my strength. I asked about Professor Aubuchon and told his location was secret but he was busy working with other scientists on the highly secret project for which his expertise was needed. I wondered if he thought of our adventures and hoped I might see him again sometime.

It was the height of the Battle of Britain in September 1940 and one night the German bombers rained death and destruction on other parts of the country. I could hear explosions though we were miles from where they struck. I thought of my fellow Englishmen under unholy attack and was grateful I was recovering in a mansion-turned-hospital in Kent. At eleven o'clock that night John made final rounds and sought me out. I was lying in the dark, looking out of the windows to the east, watching the play of searchlights trying to snare the Luftwaffe planes in their web, thankful my unborn child and I were in a safe place, at least for the time being. John drew the blackout curtains.

"Pretty bad tonight," John commented, taking my pulse, checking my blood pressure and listening to my heart. I agreed quietly. "I've been thinking," he continued, raising a hand to forestall any comment I might have made. "I realize you want your baby and I commend your intent, but have you thought of the difficulties you'll face? Where are you going to live?"

A question that I had been pondering. My aunt's apartment was in London. Her country home was too small for a child and me. My sister had married the previous autumn and was living in Scotland with her husband and a new baby. I had tentatively thought of calling her, although her husband was a strict (read narrow-minded) Presbyterian clergyman and might make my life miserable for my transgression. I hoped if worse came to worst I could convince Sarah to take my baby while I tried to serve Britain in whatever capacity possible. General Barclay had mentioned cryptology as a possibility: Certainly my days as an operative were finished.

"I'm not certain yet," I told John. "I have to think some more about it."

I glanced at his serious expression and realized when he took my hand he had given considerable thought to the matter. "Please then, Joan," he began. "listen to my suggestion. You've told me your lover is dead. There is no chance you could ever marry him. Would you consider marrying me?" I knew he could read the amazement at his suggestion while I tried to think of how to reply, but he continued quickly, "I know you don't love me, but I don't care. I think we could be happy together if we try and maybe in time you'll grow to feel the way I do."

His gaze was so kind, his face full of love and compassion. He leaned forward to kiss me gently and I heard him breath a soft, "Please, Joan. I promise I'll do everything within my power to make you happy and your baby will have a name."

Wasn't this too easy a solution to my problem? Could I accept his proposal in all honor knowing I loved Dan, would love him to the end of my life? John was so good, so kind—but I felt none of that all-consuming, overwhelming passion I had for

Dan. But what choice did I have? England was so conventional at the time, though there would probably be many a baby without marriage after the war. I wasn't brave. I wanted a name for my child and the safety of marriage, even if it were not marriage to the lover I had lost. I raised my eyes and nodded. "Yes, John, I will marry you, but only after you've thought about it some more. I don't want you to regret this later on, or for the rest of your life." Divorce was difficult if not impossible to obtain in the England of the 1940's.

John reassured me in a steady voice. "I know what I want, Joan. I want you regardless. I can accept second place in your feelings."

He kissed me tenderly and I felt nothing. Neither love nor disaffection. Nothing. I was empty of all feeling and desire. I watched him turn to leave the room, smiled as he said goodnight from the doorway then, after he left, turned again to the window with tears in my eyes, profoundly grateful for his offer, but still torn with love and longing for my dead lover. I felt disloyal to Dan but realized that was foolish. You can't betray the dead, only love and cherish their memory.

Chapter Ten

Two weeks after I left hospital, just as my waistbands were starting to become uncomfortably tight, I stood with John in his mother's garden and vowed to love, honor and cherish him until death did us part. I could with clear conscience make the last two promises. I hoped love would come eventually. I would do my best to make him happy I assured myself.

John's brother was an Anglican priest without the air of pomposity and lack of empathy for other's faults and weaknesses that I found in my sister Sarah's husband. His brother was serving as an army chaplain somewhere in the Midlands. It was he who performed the wedding ceremony.

There was a ghost that night in our wedding bed. John made gentle love to me, brought me to the peak of desire, consummated our marriage with considerable skill, but even though I tried to meet his passion, I think he knew my thoughts were on the father of my baby. I reached my climax trying to pretend it was Dan who possessed me, not this kind, good, loving husband who was beyond reproach. I felt like a cheat, despising myself for my unquenchable longings.

Marriage to John was—soothing, easy, undemanding—but did not stir my senses, probably just as well as my baby grew larger in me. I didn't know if John had told his mother about the circumstances of my pregnancy. I never asked. It was enough that she accepted me as his wife, and if she thought we had a premarital affair that was all right with me. It was from Catherine that John took his kind, loving qualities. Both of them strove to make me feel part of the family.

I had lived most of my childhood in a small village where my father taught at a public school. I understood the nuances of village life, even in war-time, and took my turn knitting and preparing refreshments for the Friday night dances held for servicemen stationed nearby. John made me stop working in the kitchen after I reached the sixth month of my pregnancy. He was not my doctor, of course; a friend of his in the nearest market town saw me and monitored my progress, but John knew well the limitations of my energy. My protests were met with the simple question, "Do you want this baby?" I was silent after that, grateful for his concern and efforts to make sure my pregnancy had no complications.

Night after night I lay quietly in his arms before sleep, trying not to superimpose the image of Dan on the presence of the dear, kind man I had married. I think, though, at times he sensed my thoughts. He would murmur words of endearment, sigh, kiss me gently and turn his back to me, pretending sleep, sleep he badly needed since he was the only doctor within a twenty-mile radius. I could feel the tension in his body and once reached out to touch his tightly clenched hands. There was nothing I could say—I encircled him with my arms and held him tightly, gratefully, my head pressed against his back as I whispered I loved him. But we both knew in our hearts it was a second-best love and at times I was torn with guilt.

It was late in autumn before the Nazi bombing raids slackened. Our little village had been spared much damage, one or two bombs landed in pastures, killing livestock, but no homes were destroyed, no lives lost. Our ancient little church, dark and damp, filled with echoes and ghosts from the past, had survived, although one stained-glass window had imploded from the concussion from a bomb-hit in a nearby field. Nights were cold, houses were never really warm, and food shortages becoming commonplace. We all tried to put on good faces and looked forward to the holidays as the one bright note in an increasingly difficult and cheerless existence.

Lost in my grief at times, moody, I knew I was full of self-pity and yet fortunate that things had worked out as they did. Several young women in the village learned they were made widows by the war and I felt a sisterhood with them. Though I told no one my story, I shared their grief but could not acknowledge mine.

Now I saw little of John. He was gone most of the day and arrived home late sometimes at eight-thirty or nine o'clock. I could see the tiredness and his great concern for his patients was written on his face. Medical supplies for civilians were increasingly difficult to obtain and he worried about older residents and the small children who lacked nutritious food and for those little Britons he purchased vitamin pills when available from our funds.

My visits to the doctor in town became a major project, due to lack of petrol and the traveling time involved. I usually went with John as he made his rounds and waited long hours for him to pick me up. John finally agreed it made more sense for him to monitor me and he checked my blood pressure and listened to the fetal heartbeat carefully, assuring me I was as healthy as a horse and the baby was fine. His doctor friend told him to bring me to his own home to stay when my time was imminent. Once in a while John would lay his face against my stomach to feel the baby's movements and assure me I was probably carrying an acrobat!

Catherine saw to it I walked at midday, if the winter permitted, and insisted on an afternoon nap, per her son's instructions. She was as kind to me as my own mother; more so, since my mother made it plain to Sarah and me her husband was her first priority. She loved her children but adored my father and made her preference known by her words and actions. He was king of the household and we his subjects. My sister and I had no problem with this; we adored him, too, for he was a warm-hearted, demonstrative man.

Catherine, however, had been widowed for many years—I think her sons were fourteen and sixteen when their father died. Like many widows, the boys were the light of her life, but she knew how much John loved me and accepted me as the daughter she had longed for, but never conceived. In short, I was watched, cosseted, spoiled and learned to quietly accept her overzealous care without complaint. Once I asked John if she had any idea of my background or adventures with British

Intelligence and he shook his head. "No, it's never been mentioned. I don't think she would believe it of you, my dear. It would only upset her."

He was right and I thought to myself she would be even more upset if she knew the true conception of the child I carried. There was no reason to tell her. John knew and had accepted it, which mattered most to me.

The holidays arrived, we went to Midnight Mass at church, we exchanged presents. I had knit a sleeveless sweater for John; his mother gave him a heavy woolen shirt. I tried my hand at a wartime steamed pudding and gave Catherine a bottle of scent my aunt had given me and I had never opened. John presented me with a couple of novels and a pretty antique pin that he found in London on one of his infrequent trips. We lazed around the whole Christmas week and somberly recognized the new year of 1941.

I was becoming increasingly large and indolent. John and I refrained from love-making—just as well, I could hardly move! I felt immense and immensely unattractive but John simply kissed me and told me I was aglow with beauty. I felt I had successfully submerged my feelings about Dan and made every effort to make John's life as happy as possible. If I didn't love him with the passion I felt for Dan, I respected and admired him and considered him my friend as well as my husband.

The end of February was surprisingly bitter, cold and icy. Snow drifted across untended village roads. Late on the night of the 20th I awoke with pains and reached over to tell John my time had arrived and did he think we should try to get to the doctor's house? He dressed hurriedly, went out to start the car, and came back in less than five minutes. Shaking his head he told me we would have to stay put, the ice was too treacherous for me to walk to the car and it was too dangerous to attempt the drive. He leaned down to kiss me and told me he would deliver the baby himself. He went up to the main house to seek the aid of his mother and carefully led her down to our cottage.

The baby came after six hours of labor. I can still recall the smile on John's face when he delivered it, another man's baby. Afterwards he told me however many births he attended, the miracle of a new baby brought joy to his heart. But there was not the elation of a new father in his expression, and when he said "You have a son, Joan," I saw the look on Catherine's face. She had immediately recognized from his expression and statement that it was not his child, but asked no questions. She simply leaned over to kiss me on the cheek and assure me, "He's beautiful, Joan, beautiful."

I lay there with my son on my breast and thanked God for his safe delivery and for the husband who had seen me through the ordeal of birth. I had been fortunate beyond belief. At that point I resolved to put my sorrow aside for the loss of Dan and try to be the wife John deserved. No more looking back.

We were happy for the short time we had together. We were young and in spite of John's long, long hours, we enjoyed each other's company, we knew each other's likes and dislikes, and if our marriage bed was not filled with moments of high passion we pleased each other and satisfied our bodies' normal longing for sexual satisfaction. I no longer thought of Dan each time John touched and made love to me. I tried my best to please him and reassure him of my love. And I did love him. But not with the all-consuming passion I had felt for Dan. I thought the memory of that love would fade over time.

Chapter Eleven

"Do you want to leave the baby and come with me to London tomorrow?" John asked one evening as I nursed my infant. I looked up in surprise and asked him why he was going.

"I need medical supplies and I want to talk to Dr. Fothingale about one of my patients. It would do you good to come along if you think you can manage it."

I thought of the offer longingly for a moment, then shook my head and thanked him, thinking of the effort it had been to get the baby on a fairly predictable schedule. I also worried about my milk and if little Johnny would accept a substitute formula. I was still quite tired from the birth and from the effort to deal with a sometimes cranky infant and figured the reward wouldn't be worth the work. "I'd like an invitation some other time, John," I told him, "But not now. It's too complicated. I think I'd be better off here at home."

"Perhaps you're right," he acknowledged. "We can do it later on, when the weather gets warmer. I wouldn't want to get stuck in London and have you frantic about the baby. I just thought you might enjoy going."

John kissed me goodbye the next morning, promising to bring the baby and me a present from London. With Johnny in my arms I waved goodbye, wishing I could be with him, but knowing my decision was wisest for the baby's sake.

Late that evening I received a phone call from the Metropolitan Police. Nazi bombers had flow over late that moonlit night and the hotel where John was booked had been completely demolished. Three survivors were pulled from the rubble and though rescue efforts continued, they doubted very much anyone remained alive under the pile of debris that had once been *The Londoner.*

I could not believe what I was hearing. It hadn't been that long ago, less than a year, that I had lost Dan and now the husband who had done everything possible to help me recover from that agonizing loss had been killed. Had I gone with him, my son would have been orphaned and would Catherine have raised him, knowing his blood was none of hers? Or would Sarah have prevailed upon her self-righteous husband to bring him into their home? In the midst of my anguish I was grateful fate had saved me for Johnny's sake.

John's clergyman brother came once again, this time to bury John in the grave-yard of the small old church in the village, to comfort his mother and console me as best he could. I wondered if he knew the truth about Johnny, either from Catherine or from John himself. I was fond of James, but found it impossible to discuss my transgression with him. He consoled me as best he could, but I suffered terribly from guilt, that I hadn't been able to love John as I felt I should.

I asked Catherine if she would stay with me for a while in our small cottage, not because I needed her, but I felt she needed my support and care. I woke many times to hear her weeping in the night and tried to comfort her as best I could. I, too, grieved but knew her loss was the greater. I knew she had loved John the best of of her two sons and his death required all her efforts to become reconciled to. I recall at one point saying I knew what it was to lose someone I loved beyond belief. Catherine looked me steadily in the eye and said quietly, without rancor, "I know about your loss, Joan, and I'm sorry. But the death of a child seems so unfair. You always expect them to live beyond your lifetime."

My gaze dropped. John must have told her about Dan and I was shamed before her struggle to accept her loss. As I started to reply she shook her head, "I don't want to know, Joan. John loved you and that was all that was necessary."

Never once in the years that followed did she question me about Johnny's father nor did her kindness and love towards us ever falter.

Many times I wondered if the information Professor Aubuchon had provided to the British been worth the efforts the government made to extricate him from the German camp.

There was no way of knowing, no one I could ask. I had been warned that phase of the operation was highly classified, top-secret, need-to-know only.

Life had settled down to a predictable routine. If there was little excitement, there was also little to fear. German air-raids had ceased, for the large part, through the end of '42 and '43 and we were all anxious for what we knew had to occur: The invasion of Fortress Europa, the annihilation of the Nazi war machine and, in the far distance it seemed, the eventual return of peace to England.

I was weeding our small vegetable garden late one September afternoon when I heard the phone ring and ran to answer it before the sound awakened Johnny from his nap. A secretary's voice asked for me and when I assured her it was I speaking she told me to hold for Colonel Jenkins of British Intelligence. Wondering what my former employer wanted of me considering the end result of my assignment to rescue the professor, I waited anxiously to find out the purpose of the call. No explanations were forthcoming. I was told to report to their headquarters no later than the day after next. I had no choice in the matter, I was told curtly. My presence was a command.

And so I learned that my lost young American lover lived and that I would see him as soon as arrangements could be made——

Chapter Twelve

The flight from England had been a long, tiring one, almost twelve hours. We stopped at Gander, Newfoundland to refuel, then undertook the last lap of the flight, landing in New York close to midday. The final approach gave the passengers an unparalleled view of the city with its giant skyscrapers and wide Hudson River, across which could be seen the flatlands of New Jersey. My seatmate, a young man attached to the consular service, had been a pleasant companion and, I suspected, more than casually interested in me. We passed the time in general conversation and I tried to avoid any explanation of why I was visiting the States other than to meet a prewar acquaintance. I wondered if he had been assigned to the seat by my friend the Colonel to assist and perhaps keep an eye on me. His story didn't ring any truer than mine.

He was kind though, and walked across the tarmac with me to the terminal, carrying my briefcase, raincoat and small hand luggage, saying he hoped we might get together while I was in the city.

"I'm not certain exactly where I'll be," I explained.

He would be pleased to see me to a hotel.

No reservations, I replied.

Then he would definitely help me to get settled. It was like having a very persistent gnat buzzing around one's ear.

I looked around the main concourse of the terminal wondering what I would do if I were not met. "I'm supposed to meet a friend," I told my gnat. "But I don't see—" There was Dan. All the things supposed to happen in novels did. My heart leapt within me, my stomach did a quick flip, I tried to catch my breath and I couldn't. I had to pause for a moment, certain that the pounding of my heart indicated my immediate demise.

Dan was wearing a light-weight wool jacket and casual trousers. As he scanned the arriving passengers I could observe his face. Tall, dark-haired, strong-featured, same wide, generous mouth, hinting of both humor and strong will, he hadn't changed greatly from my worn memories of my love. My first coherent thought was that nothing had changed, I still loved him even after five years. It might have been infatuation, but I could not separate infatuation from the surge of emotion I was feeling.

He caught sight of me, our eyes met, he smiled widely and walked toward me swiftly. Before I could say a word he had reached for me and hugged me tightly to his body. I felt his arms hold me, closed my eyes for a second—the smell of his body held me in thrall—fought back tears and knew he could feel me tremble at his touch. I laid my head on his shoulder for a second and returned his embrace. I felt his finger under my chin, lifting my head up to kiss me lightly on my cheek. "Welcome to America, Cupcake."

I smiled at him shakily. "I never thought I'd see you again in this life, Dan." From the intensity of his gaze I was certain he was feeling the same sense of wonder I did, that against all knowledge, all possibility, we were brought together again.

I realized the gnat was still by my side and stepped back to introduce him. "This is my seat companion, Evan Quinton. My friend, Daniel Childress."

Both men shook hands, smiled, how-do-you-doed, but there was tension between the two of them which secretly pleased me, for what woman doesn't enjoy rivalry, if it is on her account?

"Thank you for taking care of her, Mr. Quinton. Perhaps we will all meet each other some other time." Dan's tone was civil, but the pointed lack of cordiality was apparent to both Quinton and I.

Quinton suavely replied, "I have been instructed to see Mrs. Ferguson to her hotel and be of whatever assistance possible, Mr. Childress." Just as I suspected, Colonel Jenkins had assigned him to keep tabs on me.

"No need, Mr. Quinton, Mrs. Childress and I will be entertaining Mrs.—Ferguson while we complete our business." I noticed he hesitated over my married name. Had no one mentioned it to him. Then, the reality of his reply struck me. No one had told me *he* was married!

Quinton stood his ground. "I'll have to ask you then for an address and telephone number, Mr. Childress. We have to be able to contact Mrs. Ferguson if necessary."

After jotting down the information Quinton turned to me, handed me his card and told me to contact him when I had completed my assignment. He wished us a courteous good bye, reminded me to feel free to call him at any time, should I feel the necessity. The address on the card was the British Embassy in New York. I told him I would.

"Your bodyguard? Nanny?" grinned Dan as I laughed at his characterization. "Come on, Mrs. Ferguson, we'll get your luggage."

The light was different in New York, I thought, as I waited at the curb for Dan to bring the car around. The appearance of everything looked brilliant in the mid-day sunshine. Perhaps it was because it was so different from drab, dowdy England. I looked around. No bomb damage—well-dressed people moving at a more rapid pace than England. There was such an air of vibrancy in this, the largest city in America. I had been here as a young child with my parents, but was unable to recall much beyond the giant skyscrapers which dominated my childish impressions.

It was difficult to believe the American people had experienced the war, although I knew this was not the case. We had been inundated by their armed forces during the last year of the war and we truly could not have won without their presence. England was too exhausted, her fighting ranks too depleted, though few of us would acknowledge that aloud.

The car Dan drove amazed me. It was a big, prewar sedan and as I spotted the hood ornament I realized it was a Packard. I raised my eyebrows as Dan loaded my luggage into the backseat. "Elegant," I commented.

"It was my Dad's. It was on blocks through the war. I never would have gotten my hands on it but he passed away a year ago."

"I'm sorry," I murmured automatically. Seated. I turned to him, aching inside, to say, "Dan, I am really uncomfortable about imposing on your and your wife. I could stay at a nearby hotel."

"No hotels in Brentley, Joan. Besides, my mother, Mrs. Childress, will be a perfect chaperone if you're worried." I knew he saw my cheeks color and my expression change as he reached for my hand to squeeze it reassuringly. "Come on, let's go. We'll have lunch along the way."

I tried not to show the elation I felt when he told me he was still single and silently thanked the gods. I looked left and right as we drove out of the city, still fascinated by my first adult glance at American life. Dan concentrated on navigating his way through busy afternoon traffic. "Everything is so new looking," I marveled. "So beautiful."

"Well, compared to London, of course it is new."

"What are you doing now, Dan. What are you working at?" I assumed it would be some form of government service. His answer surprised me.

"I'm an assistant professor of American History at Guardian College. I'm working on my Ph.D. under the G.I. Bill."

I knew this was a vast, far-reaching plan which enabled American veterans to gain more education, and a host of other benefits as the nation showed its appreciation for the sacrifices their young men had made. But I would never have pictured Dan as an academic, not the quick-witted, active man I remembered, seemingly more suited to movement than studious contemplation.

"Why history, Dan?"

"Because we need to know the reasons behind the wars and events that have shaped mankind's life through the ages. Have you ever heard the adage that those who ignore history are doomed to relive it?" I nodded. "Besides, history fascinated me all through school."

I pondered his statement as we rode along. Although I knew I was too conscious of being close to him, aware of his every movement, I felt at ease with him as though the five years that had separated us was of no importance. But there was a difference. He was more mature, more certain of himself (although I remembered he had never lacked for confidence,) a quietly positive, self-assured adult. I wondered what changes he saw in me.

"I thought we'd stop for lunch before we got on the Parkway. Are you hungry?"

Tired and head-achy would have been a better description. The food on the plane was terrible and I ate very little. Maybe what I needed was something to eat. "Yes, I think I am, Dan."

We stopped at an orange-roofed, turquoise-trimmed Howard Johnson's restaurant with a sign that proclaimed "29 Ice Cream Flavors." Since I hadn't tasted even one flavor of ice cream for years, I decided that's what I'd have for dessert.

I ordered an omelet, Dan ordered something called a cheeseburger with French fries, an American delicacy, he announced gravely. Lingering over our second cup of really excellent coffee, we exchanged trivialities. I had already told him I'd explain the circumstances of our parting years ago after we discussed the reasons I had traveled to see him. He nodded, then asked the question I had been expecting, in as subtle a fashion as possible, given Dan's ability to zero in on any concern.

"Does your husband mind your leaving him for a week or so?" I sensed his tension as he waited for my answer.

"I'm widowed, Dan. John Ferguson died in 1941 as a result of a direct bomb hit on his hotel in London."

I tried to read the expression on his face as he spoke the conventional condolences then asked, "How long were you married?"

"Less than a year, September 15, 1940 to be exact." And I was three-and-a-half months pregnant with your child, I thought. Dan and I had parted early in May 1940.

His face revealed no hint of what he might be thinking, but I knew he must have felt pain at the realization I had married so soon after his supposed death.

"How did you meet?"

"I was desperately ill when I returned from my last mission. He was the doctor who attended me. He fell in love with me and proposed marriage while I was recovering." I tried to be truthful. I couldn't tell him John fell in love with me knowing all the while I was still grieving the loss of a lover. Dan quickly caught the nuance in my answer.

"He fell in love with you—and how did you feel?" His voice was low, steady, insistent.

I hated this. I answered Dan the only way I knew how. "I admired him. I grew to love him. But I was never in love with him the way I—" I stopped, unable to go on.

"Finish the sentence, Joan."

I knew he could see the tears forming in my eyes and I hoped the truth of my answer would help bridge the terrible loss of years between us. "I was never in love with him the way I loved you. Never." My voice was ragged as I tried to continue. "To tell the truth, Dan, I didn't care if I lived or died at that point. I thought I had lost you forever, and here was a wonderful man who was ready to love me and take care of me. So, I accepted his proposal. It wasn't fair to him I realized, and I told him so, but that's what I did. I tried my best to be a good wife and to make him happy."

"And was he?"

"I don't know. I hope so." I wanted to say to Dan, don't judge me, you don't know the whole story, but I couldn't. I couldn't beg for his understanding or sympathy. I was afraid he would inquire about children and quickly asked, "Dan, wasn't there anyone for you—after?"

He shook his head, "No one who ever came close to what you meant to me." His next words were a challenge, "Maybe this is a second chance."

I placed my hand on his and said gently, "Maybe. Maybe it's too soon to tell." I knew in my heart I hoped it was, but how would we ever find out, an ocean apart? We needed time, much more time.

He smiled, "Well, we'll see." His expression told me he was not rebuffed by my cautious statement.

Difficult as it was, I was glad I had to answer his questions at the onset. The facts were out in the open and I didn't have to wait to bring up the subject. I had told the truth and I hoped he believed me. As to our present feelings, we would have to sort them out in the little time we had.

I was afraid we were swept up in a tide of memories, of what might have been, rather than the present day existence of our lives. We were different people than we were in 1940, older, wiser, annealed in the fire of war. Or were we? I only knew I wanted to feel his arms around me, his kisses again, regardless of the effort I had made to place our relationship on a logical basis. I felt exactly the way I did in 1940, head-over-heels in love, heedless of the consequences. I had the feeling he could read this in my expression, even as we stood to leave the restaurant.

Chapter Thirteen

We pulled onto the Merritt Parkway and Dan told me the roadway had been built just before the war. "Look at the overpass bridges," he instructed me. "Mostly art deco, but each one is different, There's no commercial traffic, just automobiles." The Parkway was beautifully landscaped and another marvel of American design and engineering.

Perhaps to fill the void of our mutual silence Dan switched on the radio to current popular music, something called "The Make-Believe Ballroom," on a local station. Some of the music was familiar, certainly the voice of Frank Sinatra who entranced youngsters in England as well as bobby-soxers in the United States. I heard Dinah Shore's voice, then I must have dozed off because the next thing I knew we were approaching the center of a beautiful small New England town, complete with spired church and central green. The flight had been long, our conversation disconcerting, and I really hadn't slept for close to twenty-four hours. I must have turned sideways on the seat with my head resting against the back, close to Dan's shoulder. He pulled into the driveway of a large white Dutch colonial facing the green and peered down at me. "Awake?"

"Umm," I sat up and apologized. "I'm sorry. I missed the rest of the Parkway."

"You'll have a chance to see it on the way back to the airport. I'm sure the flight was tiring."

I looked at the house, so much larger than I expected. "We're here. This is your home?"

"Yes, there's my mother in the doorway."

I felt at a disadvantage, probably disheveled, without a chance to check my hair or makeup. "Do I look all right?"

Dan smiled, "You look fine." He reached over to push back a lock of hair that had fallen over my forehead and our eyes locked for the briefest of moments.

"Come on, Cupcake," and I laughed at his old chosen word of endearment. "Mom has been dying to meet you."

He took my arm as we walked up the brick walk from the driveway to the steps. I was surprised when his mother ("Call me Geraldine,") reached forward to kiss me on the cheek. I could not get used to the easy affection Americans showed to friends and strangers alike, but I liked it.

No more than five feet tall, petite, brown-haired with a streak of grey in short-cut bangs and silver sides of hair, Geraldine looked nothing like her son. "I'm so glad to meet you, Joan. I know how much you and Dan meant to each other," she said forthrightly. I smiled, genuinely liking this woman at first impression, and thanked her for the hospitality she was extending to me.

"We'll have a cocktail now and supper in about an hour or so. That will give you time to get settled and freshen up. Dan, I'll have a martini and how about you, Joan?"

I assured her that would be fine with me.

Their home was lovely, furnished with eighteenth-century mahogany reproduction furniture, largely Queen Anne in style. The rooms were well proportioned, lit by side-draped and curtained windows. The gleaning oak floors were covered in places with oriental rugs, not reproductions I was certain. There was taste and discernment displayed in the decorating.

A portrait hung over the fireplace, a silver-haired man in robes. He resembled an older Dan. "Your father?" I questioned.

"That was done about six months before he died." There was a trace of sadness in Dan's voice, but I saw love and pride in his face as he gazed at it.

"The robe?" I didn't know if it were academic or judicial. The latter.

"He was a circuit court judge."

It was like opening a new book. I had no idea of Dan's family background but it was obvious from the house and his father's position, they were comfortably well off. "You must miss him terribly."

"I do. We both do. He was a good example for a boy, very strict, but kind and decent, even to those who were tried in his court." He nodded toward the kitchen. "It's been hard on Mom. That's why I moved back after I got out of the Army I knew she was lonely, but we try to live our own lives. No apron strings, Joan."

"What did you do in the army?" I asked.

He smiled and said, "Covert operations." I later found he had been active in the OSS, but he would never discuss his work in detail.

The martinis were well mixed, the conversation light and general. I appreciated the feeling of relaxation the alcohol provided. "Such a treat," I sighed. "Life in England was— Spartan for the past five years. You cannot imagine how wonderful it is to be here. It makes me quite envious." I went on to describe some of the economies and inventiveness Britons necessarily resorted to to make life bearable.

"Use it up, wear it out, make it do," Geraldine commented, adding, "It's an old New England saying." It certainly summed up Britain's existence during the long war years up to the present. I thought about my search for various items when I was last in London.

Dinner was delicious, an entree called Yankee Pot Roast. (I would have called it braised beef) with vegetables cooked in the broth, accompanied by something called Waldorf Salad, a mix of chopped apples, nuts, raisins, celery and salad dressing and a slice of rich pound cake for the sweet. I complimented Dan's mother who said a simple "Thank you," rather than disparaging the praise which would have been a more typical English reaction.

"It's a meal that holds well if dinner is delayed," she explained. I thought I would try to duplicate it at home, if I could ever find the quantity of meat required. Maybe in a few years' time.

I was surprised when Dan stood to help his mother clear the table. I rose to help, too, but Geraldine would not allow it. "I

72

have a woman who comes in tomorrow to help," she explained. "You two go into the living room (lounge, I translated to myself) and carry on your business. I'm going to your Aunt Lydia's" she told her son. "Are the keys in the car?" Dan handed them to her with an admonition to drive carefully. Geraldine sent him a look of amused annoyance and he grinned back. "You sound like your father," she commented.

"Let's sit over here on the sofa," Dan indicated. Americans phrased things so much differently, I thought. It took me a second or two at times to translate their speech patterns. We sat side by side and the heat of his body began to stir me, although I was determined to ignore it. Did my closeness have the same effect on him I wondered?

I had brought the photograph Colonel Jenkins had provided downstairs before dinner. I opened the envelope and handed the photograph to Dan. "Do you recognize this man?"

He had a quizzical expression on his face as if to say, "You were flown over here just to have me identify a photograph?" then studied the picture intently.

"That's the French driver who drove us to the rendezvous with the plane. But he didn't look like this then."

I nodded in agreement. "That's what I said, too. But it is the same man?" I wanted to be certain of his confirmation. I handed him one of the documents I had been given which called for his arrest and trial at the Nazi war crimes tribunal, asking "Can you add anything to this indictment?"

"No—I heard him mutter a few cuss words in German while we were waiting, I admit I wondered, but since he seemed to have been cleared by your intelligence group, I assumed he was okay. What could we have done anyway?"

"You're right. Anything else you can recall at the time?"

"When the professor was taken from us I wondered if he fingered us to the guards who were probably Nazis. But at that point my only concern was to get you safely on that plane."

I knew at that moment we were in total recall, terrified we would be caught and imprisoned by the Nazis. I was praying the plane would land safely and take us back to Britain with the information that had been given me. I remembered Dan reassuring me we had done our best, but that wasn't nearly good enough for me.

I felt Dan's eyes on me as my memories swept back to that night. I heard him say, "Don't grieve, Joan. It's five years later and we won. Tell me, did anyone ever find out what happened to Professor Aubuchon? Was he killed in a camp?"

"No, I was sent back to retrieve him. That was my last mission."

"My God! Alone? What were they thinking of?" He looked furious at the thought.

"I was the only one who could identify him, remember?"

"I remember." How well I remembered. Dan reached over to grasp my hand and I took delight in his touch. "You're one brave lady, did I ever tell you that?"

I smiled. "Maybe once, a long time ago. Which brings me to the rest of the story." I drew a deep breath: How to begin?

Chapter Fourteen

I leaned back against the sofa, trying to compose myself, to collect and organize my thoughts. Again, the sense of unreality. The world was at peace, although there were rumblings surfacing from the Soviet Union. I was seated in a lovely room, still bemused by the fact that seemingly so little had touched the lives of Americans (I knew this was not true; I had seen the casualty statistics) the events I was about to talk about were five years ago, yet I was haunted by a sense of unfairness and loss, of decisions made without consultation with the participants, and the choices I had to make to keep my unborn baby.

"I had agreed to go back to France for the Professor. I really had no choice. It was a direct order, Dan. I was told the mission could not fail this time, that careful plans had been made, that I would have help every step of the way. I was to be taken into a heavy labor camp, contact the professor and await developments. I was terrified. I have never been as afraid as I was then."

He was intent on my face, listening closely as I told him that the powers-to-be had decided it would be best if we disappeared, that our names were listed in Nazi files. We were, in effect, killed. I told him about the false manifest listing our names as being killed in the crash of one of the Pan Am Clippers flying to Lisbon.

"I was told you died on that flight, Dan. That the plane had been shot down. Who would doubt British Intelligence? I certainly didn't. We were simply pawns in their greater plan, with no regard for our feelings. What were you told?"

His face was grim, echoing my feelings of bitterness. "The US Embassy told me the same thing, that you had been killed on another flight. I didn't doubt it either. Remember, I had no idea of your assignment." I heard the regret and anger in his voice, then he asked, "How did you finally get the Professor out?"

I shuddered. "It was horrible, Dan. The worst experience of my life. We were both placed in the bottom of a hand-cart used to carry the dead to burial pits ten minutes before the bodies were collected. Our rescuer threw a tarp over us saying he would tell the graves detail we were left over from the night before and beginning to decompose. He yanked the tarp off when the truck came with that day's dead and soldiers began throwing the bodies on top of us. We could hardly breath from their weight. We couldn't move a muscle."

I buried my face in my hands, unable to continue for a moment. "Oh, Dan, the bodies were cold, so cold. They were naked as we were. They pressed down on us, a tangle of legs, arms, babies, children and women. Human beings treated like refuse. They had had lives like us, snuffed out with no remorse."

My hands were clasped tightly on my lap, eyes closed, reliving the horror of that escape. Dan reached for me, drew me close to him, saying over and over, "I'm sorry, Joan. I'm so sorry. I never should have asked."

I could smell his aftershave lotion, I felt the warmth of his body, the strength of his arms, the comfort of his whispered words and fought to regain my composure. His hands caressed my hair, held my shoulders tightly, and I knew instinctively he wanted to kiss me but would not. Passion would not assuage my grief, not at this moment, and perceptively he realized it. There was an expression of total pity on his face and perhaps helplessness. He shared my grief by listening, but knew only I could deal with it. I thought I had, long ago, but now realized I had only buried it. He held me close for a few minutes more, then, in an attempt to distract me asked in a husky voice (was he having trouble with his feelings, too?) if I wanted to sit in on his early American History class. "Assistant Professors get the eight o'clock lectures," he explained ruefully.

Of course I wanted to and told him so. What, I asked, was the topic. Events leading up to the American Revolution, freedom from British tyranny, he grinned. I smiled slightly, refusing to rise to the bait.

That reminded me of one item of business I hadn't addressed yet. "Is there a place called Lake Tonionga far from here? Have you heard of it?

"Yes, it's about an hour's drive or so. Why?"

I explained that I owned a cottage there that had been left to my father before the war by his cousin. I had inherited it and for years had rented it out through a real-estate agent who handled all necessary repairs and billed me for them. "I'd like to see what it's like and what condition it's in, especially since I would have you to advise me. I don't know if I want to keep it or not."

"Okay, we can leave after class, eat when we get there. Maybe Mom can lend you a bathing suit. It might be warm enough to swim."

I was dubious, but agreed it might be.

I stifled a yawn, not too successfully. I was exhausted after coping with the day's events. Dan poured a pony of brandy for each of us, lifted his glass and suggested we drink to peace. It was as good a toast as any, considering how much we had sacrificed to achieve it.

I don't know what time it was when I awakened, unable to move, caught in the terror of a nightmare. I probably had moaned or called out because suddenly Dan was leaning over my bed. I could not see his face in the dark, but heard his voice whisper my name. I had been dreaming about the bodies piled on top of me at the labor camp. So real was it I could feel the terrible, terrible coldness they exuded. I began to shiver uncontrollably. I felt Dan's arms lifting me up to hold me closely, murmuring, "I'm here. It's all right. You're safe, Joan, you're safe."

I clung tightly to him, finally fully awake, dimly aware he had only pajamas on and I a thin silk nightgown. Did I feel the light pressure of his lips on my forehead? Suddenly a molten wave of desire swept over me. I could not judge the degree of his arousal in the dark but from his quickening breath and the pressure of his encircling arms I judged him to be as full of longing as I was. He groaned softly and tilted my head back to kiss me. I felt his tongue against my teeth, opened my mouth to trace my tongue along the side of his. We had not touched elsewhere but I was frantic, abandoned to all the latent passion he aroused in me. We quickly drew apart as we heard his mother speak outside the door. "Dan, is Joan all right? I thought I heard her cry out"

Dan swore under his breath and told her it was only a nightmare. "It's okay, Mom. Go back to bed."

Mom probably had her doubts but she said, "Good night then," sweetly, probably figuring there was little she could do to protect our virtues. But the spell was broken, probably for the best. Dan quickly kissed me again on the lips, hugged me once more and asked him if I wanted him to stay until I fell asleep.

"Go back to bed," I told him. "You have to lecture tomorrow." Then I said softly, "Thank you, Dan. I was so frightened." Until you kissed me. He was briefly silhouetted against the hall light as he closed the door.

I lay awake until I could see the sky lighten. I still had fears about any relationship we might resume but I knew I wanted him regardless. I remembered saying to him, was it only yesterday? "Time will tell—" then I drifted off, for an hour or two of fitful sleep.

When I awoke there was no longer any conflict in my mind. I loved him and would tell him so before I returned to England. Then it would be up to him. No more shilly-shallying. No more worrying about lapsed time. How it would end, I was uncertain, but at last I was certain of my feelings. And, I thought, I was certain of his—I hoped.

Chapter Fifteen

I didn't know what to wear to a college lecture. I finally settled on the suit I had worn on the plane with a different blouse. I checked to see I had a small notebook in my purse in case I wanted to make notes of some of Dan's comments. I had trouble picturing him as a professor. I myself had no academic degree. After I left school I had assisted my father in recording data involving his experiments.

I dressed quickly and tip-toed downstairs. I heard clatter in the kitchen and smelled coffee brewing. Geraldine was beating eggs as I peeked into the kitchen and I also thought I could smell bacon. Neither Dan nor his mother could know how much I enjoyed the food they served. I tried not to be a glutton but I could have devoured everything set on the table, especially after years of war-time austerity. I felt uneasy as I greeted Geraldine who turned to me with a smile. "Everything looks and smells so good," I ventured. She laughed and I braced myself for my next sentence. "Uhh, Geraldine, about last night—"

She shook her head and responded reassuringly, "Joan, don't. No explanations. None are necessary." At that point Dan entered, short-sleeve shirt, bow-tied, looking as tired as I was. "Did you finally get to sleep?" he questioned. I told him I had.

After we ate Geraldine handed me a bathing suit and towels saying she hoped it would fit. I could feel the heat of an early autumn sun already shining through the curtained windows in the breakfast nook. Perhaps we might be able to swim at the lake. We could ask the real estate agent if it were permissible.

As Dan picked up his brief case Geraldine kissed him on the cheek and hugged me. "Enjoy your day. Call me if you can't be home for supper."

She must be lonely, I thought. Her husband hadn't been gone for long and I knew the pain she must be experiencing. I wondered how she would feel about losing Dan and then realized I was being presumptuous.

The college where Dan taught was in town, not more than two miles away. "Close enough to bike to," he commented as he parked his gigantic vehicle in a numbered space. "I have a small section this semester, but when the GI's get back, this place will be jumping." He collected his notes, slipped on a jacket and we set off across the campus.

Guardian College was a small liberal arts school, Dan told me, a mixture of architectures: a turn-of-the-century mansion which housed administration and some classrooms, two more modern buildings, the science building and the library; several dormitories, also built early in the century, with curved glass windows in the end towers. The grounds were carefully tended. Other buildings were set further back close to a grove of tall trees.

Dan's class was composed mostly of young women with one or two bespectacled boys in attendance, I assumed because so many soldiers were waiting to be demobbed. Pretty girls, long shiny hair in pageboy bobs, sat wearing plaid skirts with Peter Pan-collared blouses and oversized cardigans around their shoulders. Most wore brown and white saddle shoes. They chattered together nervously, like magpies, until Dan stepped to the podium. The girls in the front row focused intensely on him, turning to each other to giggle, and I thought to myself they have crushes on him. The class fell silent as Dan began to lecture, the only sound was that of feet occasionally shuffling and the scratch of fountain pens as notations were made of dates and events mentioned.

He was a good speaker. I was fascinated—not much information had been given as to the reasons for the American Revolution when I was in school. It was treated as a minor event. Evidently the high-handedness of England's taxation of her colonies was a crucial grievance as well as the lack of recognition of their efforts to gain representation in Parliament. When a hand was occasionally raised. Dan stopped to answer the student's question. He was witty, articulate and well-versed in his subject.

When the class started he had introduced me as an old wartime friend from England and at one point asked me if I cared to share any comments with the class. I shook my head, saying only that I supposed the distance between England and the New World caused great problems in communication. "Very true, and seldom recognized," Dan acknowledged.

One or two girls spoke to him after class, questioning something about a term paper, whatever that was. I intercepted a couple of curious glances sent my way, smiled, and as the class departed I stood, waiting for Dan to gather his papers scattered about the podium. I was interested in the American style of lecturing large groups of students in a classroom setting rather than the tutorial system in England.

"I can't tell you how much I enjoyed your lecture, Dan. You held everyone's attention. I learned a great deal," I praised him. I was impressed with this facet of his personality and the quick intelligence he displayed.

We stopped by his office to pick up some test papers after his lecture. It was a tiny little room, desk, chair, chair the other side of the desk for visitors or students; bookcases, jammed with books, books everywhere, some piled up on the floor behind the desk. "Organized disorder," Dan stated with a smile. It reminded me of my father's desk so long ago, especially the smell of leather book bindings and the dust motes that rose as Dan sorted through papers on his desk.

As we walked back to his car I turned to glance around once again at the setting. Secure, peaceful, a sense of permanency. I could easily understand the appeal of the academic life, its orderly progression from semester to semester, year to year.

"You've chosen a good life for yourself, Dan," I commented as we drove off. "Personal satisfaction and the knowledge you'll influence your students' lives and outlook."

"I hoped you would like it," was all he replied.

I wondered, though, if there was room for an English woman in this new world and in his life. Would we be able to surmount out differences in upbringing and attitude? And, always present in my mind, the fact we had a child he was unaware of. What would Dan's reaction be to that?

Lunch was at an Italian restaurant close to Lake Tonionga. I discovered antipasto was a large salad, almost a meal in itself, followed by lasagna, an unfamiliar but delicious entree. We sopped up sauce with crusty Italian bread. I declined dessert, but asked for coffee, aware I had overeaten this wonderful stateside food, a constant state of affairs I realized guiltily.

"You haven't asked for tea yet," Dan observed with a smile.

I told him the coffee in the United States was the best I had ever tasted and I couldn't resist it.

"It's our reaction to dumping all that taxed tea in Boston Harbor. We decided to boycott it after that." I took his statement in good faith, then saw the twinkle in his eye.

Mr. Dreyfuss was the real estate agent I had been corresponding with through the years. He turned out to be sandy-haired, stocky, middle-aged and alone in his office. He apologized for not driving us to my cottage but explained he had another client to see. He handed me the key and gave Dan directions. We could drop the key through the mail slot if he was not there when we finished and call him the next day with any questions or decisions I might have reached.

We found the cottage down a dirt road. Small, maybe two rooms, porch overlooking the lake. I glanced up to see power lines leading to the house. Before entering, we walked around the outside to check the roof. "Needs replacing," Dan noted, and a coat of paint would have improved the exterior appearance. The downspouts were in place, but the gutters were full of leaves. "They should be cleaned out," I was advised.

I was glad to have the benefit of his observant eyes and advice, although I was accustomed to trying to maintain my English cottage.

The key opened the door without difficulty and I remembered our first meeting in Paris where I struggled to open my hotel room door only to be assisted by a good-looking young American who would change my whole life.

We entered into a living room/kitchen arrangement with a bedroom and tiny bath off to one side. The front porch was screened and three cots covered with a tarpaulin formed an alcove at one end of the porch, either for sleep or a sitting area, I supposed. Furnishings were sparse. A brass bed with a sagging mattress in the bedroom, small bureau, night-stand, over-head light. The rooms smelled musty with that damp, humid air prevalent to all lakeside homes. Two overstuffed, badly faded chairs in the living room sat across from a wooden settee, one end table, one floor lamp; an oak table and four chairs resided near the minimal, miniscule kitchen. There was a pump at the kitchen sink, no running water, no water heater, but I lived with the same conditions in my English cottage.

I stood surveying the room, indecisive as to whether I should keep the cottage or not. It had produced no income through the war years; it was unlikely I would travel to American to use it in the summer. "I'm not sure exactly what I should do about this," I told Dan. "It's been rented out, but the agent has kept an eye on things. There's no vandalism or damage. What do you think, Dan? Should I keep it?"

He looked around speculatively. "There's going to be a terrific housing shortage when the G.I.s get back. You might think about winterizing it and renting it out all-year round. I could keep an eye on it for you." He opened french doors to the porch. "Come out and look at the view."

It was lovely. Across from us was a spit of land which effectively would shelter the cottage from winds sweeping across the lake. There were houses to be seen on the right, far down the lake, empty now that children were back in school. Rowboats were pulled up far above the waterline. I looked, but evidently no boat belonged to this house.

It was quiet, peaceful. A couple of tall maple trees' leaves cast dappled shadows over the porch and a slight sigh of wind drifted through the trees as we stood there. We could see the beginning of autumn in the traces of color on the nearby trees and those across the lake.

"Why don't we put on our bathing suits and see what the water's like?" Dan suggested. "If it's too cold, we won't go in."

I was less than enthusiastic but thought we could try. To my surprise the water was far warmer than any I had experienced in England. Even in those long ago childhood days at the beach we rarely ventured in beyond our knees.

I just managed to fit into Geraldine's bathing suit. A wartime diet heavy on starches and the food I had gluttonously devoured the last day or so made me too aware of the tightness around my waist. I glanced at myself in the dim mirror over the bureau and realized motherhood, too, had made me very dissatisfied with my appearance. But, when I stepped out of the bedroom into the living room I heard a low wolf-whistle from Dan and saw his eyes sweep up and down my figure with an appreciative grin.

My heart caught in my throat as I looked at him. Tall, well-proportioned, wide-shouldered, still flat-stomached—I felt the urge to move close into his arms to kiss and be kissed. He was a handsome, desirable man and I knew he was aware of it from the confident attitude he presented. It wasn't arrogance; it was sheer male allure.

I turned to reach for my towel to break the seductive spell I was under, afraid I would make a fool of myself, reveal the need I felt to feel his touch, his caress. I thought the air vibrated with our mutual unexpressed desire as Dan followed me down the path to the tiny sandy beach, almost stalking me like an animal ready to claim his mate. My fancy created a tingling warmth throughout my body.

I breast-stroked out fifty or so feet and to my right saw Dan cutting through the water with a powerful crawl. Just ahead I could see the flat top of a rock breaking through the surface of the water and I swam towards it, wondering if we could find a foothold large enough for both of us to stand on to rest. We stood close together, bodies almost touching and I felt warmth and slowly building excitement as we stood there. Dan's eyes were dark, intense as he reached for me to hold me steady, his voice thick, husky as he told me to hold on to him. I smiled, turned, slipped into the water and began to swim back to shore, glancing over my shoulder provocatively, challenging him to follow me without words. But this time, no mindless engagement of our bodies. I wanted commitment, marriage, no possibility of reliving my experience as an unwed mother. I watched him as I briskly toweled myself and saw him draw a deep breath and struggle to regain control.

We stood there, side by side, looking over the lake. Suddenly Dan pointed upward. "Look up, Joan. There's a bald-headed eagle."

I turned but couldn't see the bird at first. Dan put his arm around my shoulder and pointed to the left. I could see the bird gliding down toward the top of a fir tree standing tall against the sky, its huge nest anchored to the very top branches. We watched it land then effortlessly Dan turned me back towards his body saying, "Let's keep the cottage, Cupcake. It'll be a good place to bring the kids."

For a moment I didn't grasp what he was saying, then he leaned down, drew me against him and asked, "Will you marry me? I promise I'll love you always." I heard myself answer "yes" without hesitation and reached up to meet his kiss, more gentle and controlled than I expected. If I had to describe our feelings I think exultation would be the closest to expressing the joy we felt after so many years of anguish and longing and loneliness. We kissed again, not with the passion of the night before, but in anticipation of the joy we would experience in the future.

"I have research to do in England for my Ph.D., Joan," Dan was saying, "Even though we'll live here, we'll have a summer to spend over there, probably next year."

At that point I didn't care if I never saw England again. The only thing important to me was how would I tell Dan of Johnny? It had to be done now, in all fairness to the man I promised to marry. I took his hand to lead him up to the cottage. "Let's change, Dan. Then I have something to tell you."

85

Dressed, we sat side by side on the battered settee as I reached for my purse. I slipped Johnny's photograph out of a leather holder and handed it to him. "You have a son, Dan. This is Johnny. He's four-and-a-half years old."

The expression on Dan's face was a mixture of incredulity and happiness. I think it took him a minute to fully absorb what I was telling him, then he reached over to take me in his arms again.

"I never stopped to think that night in London—Oh, Joan, I never—is that why you married John?" I could see guilt and concern written on his face.

I nodded, realizing I was presenting Dan a fait accompli, that we had conceived Johnny the first night we slept together. How would he feel about this? Would the prospect of unexpected fatherhood give him pause to think, to turn away from me? I tried to hide my anxiety as I watched him study the photograph, then glance up at me as if cataloguing our son's features in his mind. His mouth and jaw, my eyes and coloring. I saw tears in his eyes, his hand raised quickly to shield his expression from my gaze. I reached out to touch his cheek, wipe away a tear or two that had escaped—tears of joy, tears of pride, I hoped.

"You will never know how much I wanted our baby, Dan," I whispered. "I was so afraid I would lose him in the prison camp. I was fortunate John wanted to marry me, but I never considered any other alternative. I couldn't." I reached out to him and when his arms encircled me I heard a muffled, "Thank you." It was more than enough assurance that he accepted his sudden fatherhood as a gift I brought him, not a totally unexpected burden he had to accept.

Chapter Sixteen

Nuremberg was the final chapter in World War 11, at least for us. For those who suffered directly from the results of Hitler's attempt to conquer Europe, England and Russia, it provided some vindication for the immense suffering people endured. Some vindication. There could never be justice or satisfaction for the six-million jews who died in concentration camps, or lost families or children, or for the brave soldiers maimed, wounded, or missing in action; families torn asunder, property and prized possessions lost forever in the debris and destruction of war.

What infuriated many was the fact that only a few Nazi war criminals were hanged; thousands were sent to prison but received far lighter sentences than expected; however, their perfidy and cruelty was exposed world-wide and perhaps that provided some satisfaction to those who survived the Nazi crimes against humanity.

Dan and I both testified that the man Colonel Barclay called Dieter had assisted in the capture of Professor Aubuchon and had betrayed us to the Nazis. We confronted him face to face and I took great satisfaction in aiding in his conviction. Events would not have been changed, I know. It was British Intelligence who decided we had to be eliminated and deaths certified, but I would never forget the terror of that night we flew out of France over the English Channel, nor would I forgive Dieter for my having to return to Europe to bring the Professor out of the concentration camp at what might have easily been the loss of my unborn child's life.

Dieter was imprisoned for five years, and I wondered later if he had served the complete sentence, or had been released earlier. I stared him in the eye at the end of his sentencing and shuddered at the chilling, remorseless look he gave Dan and I.

After our testimony I returned to England with Dan. I had spoken to Catherine the day before and told her I was bringing an old war-time friend back with me. It was a cold, clear, crisp late autumn day when we got off the train and I asked Dan if he would mind walking the half mile to the cottage, explaining gas was still in very short supply. We carried overnight cases and left our suitcases with the stationmaster to be delivered that evening when he drove by our home. As we trudged up the graveled driveway the door opened and Catherine smiled a greeting. I introduced Dan and she said quietly, "I know who Dan is. He's Johnny's father, isn't he?" She turned to Dan and stated, "He looks very much like you, except for his coloring and Joan's eyes. Welcome, Dan. How wonderful you two could find each other again."

She was an amazing woman, to have known all along my son was not her grandchild by blood, and yet love and care for us without comment or question.

"How long have you known, Catherine?" I questioned, finding it difficult to meet her gaze. I had felt shame for many years over my deception and, of course the longer it continued, the more difficult it seemed to explain or talk about. "Did John tell you when we were married?"

She shook her head. "Never a word, Joan. I knew it the night your baby was born. Do you recall he said, 'You have a baby boy, Joan?' Not 'We have a son or child.' I never questioned him—I believed it was your secret and your marriage. You were a good wife and that's all that mattered to me." She turned to Dan, "But I know she thought of you many times. I could read it in her expression—a certain look of sadness she could never hide."

She reached up to touch his cheek, this usually undemonstrative Englishwoman. "Welcome again, Daniel. Next, we have to find your son, but before we do, how are you going to handle this for his sake? How are you going to explain it to a four- year old who thinks his father died in an air-raid in London during the war?"

Dan and I had discussed how we would approach this problem. We planned on simply telling Johnny that we were going to be married and that John and I would be going to America to live and that Dan would be his father. It seemed most simple to have Dan formally adopt Johnny in the United States and at a later date try to explain everything to him when he was old enough to understand. At what age a child could understand love outside the framework of marriage was problematical, but we would face that when it proved necessary. In the meantime, the three of us sat chatting nervously, waiting for Johnny to wake up from his nap and greet us. I glanced over at Dan who looked tense, even as he spoke to Catherine, telling her of his vocation as a college professor. I was certain he was apprehensive about the impending meeting with his son.

Johnny finally came downstairs, rubbing one sleepy eye, then running over to me, to hug and kiss me. "Mummy, where were you? I missed you. I thought you'd never get back." I wrapped my arms around him, watching Dan's face across the room, seeing his delighted reaction to the sight of his son. I gently turned Johnny around to face his father and said, "Johnny, this is my old friend Dan whom I've brought to meet you. Will you say hello?"

Easily Dan said, "Hi, Johnny, I'm glad to meet you," with an outstretched hand for Johnny to shake. His smile was warm and voice soft, "Can you guess where I'm from? I'm an American. I live in a little town in the state of Connecticut and I'm a teacher. Would you like to hear more about it?" He patted his knee and without hesitation, Johnny climbed up on his lap. I turned to Catherine and thought, "That's it. Let them sink or swim together now. I can't do anything more." Catherine smiled at the two of them and I was encouraged that perhaps we could sort out our differences and become a family.

"Come and help me make tea," Catherine requested and I stood, wondering what she would say to me alone in the kitchen.

We assembled the tea things in silence, I trying to overhear the on-going conversation in the parlor. I heard Dan's voice speaking slowly to Johnny and our son's excited replies and questions. Catherine watched me and asked, "How much longer will you be here?" I noted the sadness in her voice and knew she was only now facing the prospect of lonely times ahead.

"Dan has to be back to classes at his college next week," I replied. "I would really like to be married before he goes, but I don't know if we can manage that. If not, I'll follow along as soon as I can and we'll be married in Connecticut." I drew in a ragged breath as I continued. "I want you to be at our wedding, Catherine, if you would come." I held my breath, wondering if this was the last thing she wanted to do, but she smiled and told me she would, though she wasn't sure she could manage the trip to the States. "We'll have to talk. Perhaps James could perform the ceremony, if you wish." James was John's cleric brother and I was uncertain if I wanted him to marry us. Somehow I felt as though I would be betraying John's memory by doing so. "We'll see," I replied.

In the meantime, father and son were fast becoming friends. I saw Dan grin to himself as Johnny asked about the proximity of cowboys to Connecticut, a very civilized area, I thought, from my brief acquaintance with it. Gravely, he assured Johnny that although they weren't in the immediate area there were places where people took holidays and had the opportunity to ride and explore the outdoors. "Dude ranches" he called them, whatever they might be. It didn't sound like fun to me. Johnny nodded understandingly.

Dan asked if Johnny would show him around the yard and perhaps take a little walk with him so he could see the countryside, glancing over at me for approval. I could see Johnny was anxious to escort his new friend around and nodded assent with a smile. "Not too long, John" I cautioned. "Tea will be ready shortly." I would have given anything to be privy to their conversation, but knew it was best that I stay with Catherine while they became closer.

"How did it seem to find Dan after all these years?" Catherine questioned. "Did you know you were going to see him when you flew over?" There was no accusation in her words, merely interest. I said yes, but the prime reason for the trip was to identify a Nazi war criminal, not to resume a relationship I thought I had successfully convinced myself was over long ago.

"But it was as if we had never parted, Catherine," I told her. "The moment I saw him I knew I still loved him, would always love him." I told her I meant no disloyalty to John, but could never expunge Johnny's father from my heart. She nodded. There was no disapproval in her expression. I realized as a woman she understood my feelings and I wondered if there had been someone in her life before she married that had meant as much to her. I would never know nor inquire.

Dan's mother Geraldine had been welcoming, but Catherine was the mother-in-law who had sustained and comforted me for five long years and I knew I would hold her dear to me for the rest of my life. Geraldine, with all her graciousness and ready acceptance, had yet to prove herself to me. Or, to be honest—I had yet to prove myself to her. Surely she would resent the interloper who had suddenly appeared on the scene and preempted her son's love and attention. I hoped we would become close after our marriage, but I knew I would never, never forget Catherine.

Chilly twilight air entered the cottage behind Dan and Johnny. I searched Dan's face for his thoughts and saw love and gratitude there. "You've done a good job, Joan. He's a wonderful little boy." He shook his head and I knew he could find no other words to express himself at that moment.

Our marriage was accomplished with my dour brother-in-law kindly consenting to perform it, accompanied by questions, warnings and hinted-at expressions of distaste. When we told him of our miraculous reunion he murmured "Sweet is a grief well ended," a comment, he explained, made by Aeschylus, a Greek poet who lived 500 years BC. Dan nodded, recognizing the quote. Not to be outdone, I nodded too, but the allusion was lost on me.

I thought David would be pleased his fallen-woman sister-in-law would finally be made an honest wife, but that statement he failed to inject into our premarital instruction. Nevertheless, the day was fine and the tiny front room of the cottage—the scene of so much pain, some joy, and five years of austere living—was crowded with my soon-to-be former mother-in-law, Johnny, my sister Sarah who looked worn and overworked but delighted by the occasion, and the groom and I. Our eyes held each other as we repeated our vows and swore our love, both conscious that whatever enabling grace existed had permitted us to finally embark on the course we had planned at the onset of the war.

Together we had carefully explained to Johnny that we would be flying to America the next day to begin a new life, and that Dan would be his daddy. He seemed accepting, fascinated by Dan's stories of the States and the wonderful things boys could do there. Up to that point his life had been bounded by two women, a small village, the occasional village child sought out by myself and one or two other young mothers of my age, and long walks about the countryside with me or Catherine. I had no idea myself of what our life would be like in the United States, but trusted Dan's words that we would find a variety of possibilities in campus life and the beautiful Connecticut town I'd seen briefly.

I must admit I was apprehensive leaving the country I had lived in all my life for the New World. Even though I adored my new husband, who was the man I hadn't known for the past five years, and would we be able to sustain the love we felt for each other? Would I fit into an academic existence I knew nothing of? And, most importantly, could we provide Johnny with the sort of existence that would provide love, guidance and the permanency I knew he needed. All these thoughts swirled through my mind as we flew the endless hours to the United States. I wondered if Dan was entertaining second-thoughts and turned to see the expression of love on his face as he held his sleeping son. That was reassurance in itself, I felt.

We landed in a blustery snowstorm, our turbulent end to our flight had induced sickness in Johnny and I was queasy myself.

It was a pale, sickly trio met by Geraldine who had to cope with icy roads on her trip into the city to fetch us. Her greeting was affectionate to me, loving to Dan, but I saw the tears in her eyes when she hugged Johnny. "I'm going to be your grandmother," she announced to the boy who nodded, slightly bewildered by everything. Oddly enough, up to that point, I had thought of Catherine as my son's grandmother, but knew this was truly Geraldine's designation and sensed her fulfillment and joy as she met with her grandson. Her whispered thank you to us assured me Johnny and I were now accepted as kinfolk.

"How did the wedding go?" she asked as we drove up the Parkway, I told her I had worn a prewar dress that had been my mother's and that my brother-in-law had performed the ceremony. "I'd like to hold a reception for you both, Joan, so our friends and family can meet you." She added rather tentatively, "Maybe in a month or so, after you get settled."

Settled? I had no idea where we would live. Suddenly I was overwhelmed by the myriad of items we had not discussed, I had not even considered, and the fact that I would have to cope with them in a new country where I had no idea of the ways or customs.

Geraldine must have sensed my concern for she assured me she would help where possible and we would deal with Daniel together. She reached over to squeeze Johnny's hand (he sat in the front seat with Dan, eagerly watching out the car window) and stated, "Johnny will help us too, won't you? We have to find some playmates for him as soon as possible." I tried to be grateful for her assurances but wondered how much unwanted help I might get. I thought of my mother's description of *her* mother-in-law, "give her an inch and she'll take a mile." Was this going to be true of Geraldine?

It had been a long flight, the weather was colder than England, and Johnny was exhausted and probably apprehensive about this new experience. I put him to bed, asked Geraldine if she would like to read him a good-night story, a request eagerly accepted, and said I would be up to kiss him goodnight and tuck him in. I suspected he would drop off almost immediately and Geraldine would see to his needs. I was right and she came downstairs later with a smile to kiss me and tell me how wonderful her grandchild was.

Dan's mother was a take-charge person. That evening, after dinner and seeing we were settled in the guest bedroom, she announced she was thinking of moving to the west coast of Florida. Her other sister Grace lived there, was widowed and lonely and Geraldine thought it would be good if they were near one another. We could have the house to live in, she informed us, and it would provide a place for her to return to from the scorching Florida summers. I had no idea of how tight the housing shortage was in America, though Dan had mentioned it at my cottage on the lake, or I would have been more effusive about her offer. It was generous and Dan reached over to hug his mother and thank her.

We went to bed early and fell asleep, arms around each other. I lay there for a few minutes worrying about our future and feeling inadequate and anxious, wondering if we had made a mistake marrying so soon. I knew my doubts were the result of tiredness and the let-down feeling after the frantic two weeks past and hoped we would be able to deal with the small problems that were ahead of us. Maybe the big problems, too, but I couldn't pinpoint exactly what they might be. Dan's lips brushed my cheek and I heard him whisper, "Go to sleep. We'll talk tomorrow and decide what we're going to do." I squeezed his hand and drifted off.

Dan had one more day before returning to classes and we spent it exploring the town and the college campus with Johnny, who was wide-eyed at the students, the stores, seemingly packed with items he had never seen, and the wide American streets. The snow was banked against the sides of the roads and already we could see signs of Christmas in the store windows. Dan asked me if English children knew about Santa Claus and I told him we referred to him as Father Christmas. "Christmas trees?" he questioned hopefully. Not since the war began, at least not

94

with lights. I could see Johnny's father was planning on an extravaganza for our first American Christmas, although he said ruefully we had to deal with Thanksgiving first. I vaguely remembered that had something to do with the first settlers in the country—was it Plymouth? Was that in Massachusetts? How did Americans ever learn to spell these strange names?

I had read in the newspapers about the laying off of war workers and fears of inflation as pent-up demand for consumer goods created a black market. Waiting lists for new cars were 10-months to a year long, Dan told me, and we were doubly appreciative of the elegant Packard in our garage. I hadn't driven much, except for occasional runs to drop off decoded messages, and wondered if I would find it difficult to adjust to right-hand side driving. When I mentioned that Dan pulled the car over to the side of the road and told me to take it home. I did and found it felt natural after a couple of miles. I was pleased when he complimented me on my skill.

`We passed by rows of what looked to be council housing—attached homes, eight or ten in a row. When I asked about them Dan told me they were hastily erected veteran's housing, not nearly enough to supply demand, and that there was also a long waiting list for them. They comprised two bedrooms, a small living room with a kerosene heater, a "space heater" he called it, a tiny kitchen with room for a small dining table, bathroom, limited closet space, but adequate for wives who had lived with in-laws all through the war and were delighted to have their own home with their children and husbands. On lines behind the house were rows and rows of nappies (I soon learned to call them diapers) and scores of toddlers being watched over by their mothers. I smiled and wondered if we too would be parents again in the near future.

I was amazed to see gigantic foodstores, supermarkets I wrote to Catherine and my sister about, filled with unimaginable amounts of canned goods, fresh greens, massive amounts of cleaning supplies and endless supplies of meat which one obtained by telling the butcher behind the counter what you wanted for the week and seeing it shortly appear on the counter top.

.Americans might bemoan shortages of consumer goods and costs, but I considered them far less inconvenienced than what we had to endure in England. One of the first things I did was to ship a box of foodstuffs, clothing and shoes to Catherine. Immensely grateful, her reply was ecstatic and I felt it such a small thing to do for all her kindness and consideration to me in years' past. More packages were shipped out at intervals for the next few years.

Geraldine, who loved to organize, asked me if I would be amenable to a small reception the first weekend in December. The small reception turned out to be 75 to 100 people who crowded the main reception hall at the college and comprised faculty members, townspeople, neighbors and local dignitaries who were anxious to see who had finally captured the heart of their local boy. My head was spinning as I greeted people, realizing it would be months before I could sort out the names and faces.

Dan introduced me to a young female Anthropology professor named Janet who wished me a lifetime of happiness then turned to Dan, smiling, to kiss him on the cheek and congratulate him on his bride. I returned the warmth of her smile but watched the interchange closely. I felt something significant had existed between the two of them but resolved never to question Dan about it. I realized I liked Janet, there was a warmth and directness about her I found appealing, but wondered about their past history.

So much to discuss, so much to learn, so much to accept graciously. I was tense and ill at ease, as much as I tried to hide it, and wondered if Dan sensed my anxiety. I think he did, although he never referred to it directly, but when we whispered to each other in bed at night he assured me of his love and pride in me, and, at that stage of our marriage, reinforced it by his ardor when we made love. Deeply satisfied by his ministrations, I would have purred if I could have managed it.

During the day I helped Caroline with her preparations for the holiday season, discussed with her her planned exodus to Florida (not with any degree of confidence—I just knew about where the state was on the map) and was grateful for her acceptance and seeming lack of curiosity. We had explained the terrible plot to presumably keep us safe and she nodded in comprehension. The next day she told me, "I heard Dan weeping a few times at night, Joan. He loved you so much and couldn't accept your death." She signed, "It's terrible when you can't hold a grown son in your arms and comfort him."

Once again, I was grateful to the gods for reuniting us. I heard stories around me of wives and husbands who met again after the war and found they had nothing in common, no desire to make a life together, victims of the same sort of wartime passion which had swept over Dan and me. I hoped we would be lucky and able to build on our essential love for each other and not fall prey to disillusion and disinterest.

Invited to attend the annual faculty party at the college, I stood in front of our closet and tried to decide what I could possibly wear for the occasion. Aside from the few items British Intelligence had permitted me to purchase, there was very little suitable for the occasion. Add to that that the "New Look" was coming in, (long dress lengths and padded hips in some extreme cases) I was at a loss. I decided I would have to ask Dan for permission to buy an ensemble when, wonder of wonders, he read my mind and handed me a check telling me to go buy what I needed. It was a handsome amount and I knew I could probably purchase two or three outfits to carry me through the holidays and winter. I had worn my wedding dress to the reception—a timeless, dateless Worth frock which my stylish London aunt had presented my mother for some special event before the onset of war.

Geraldine and I set out the next day to shop after Dan returned from classes to watch Johnny. I had enjoyed my trip to Harrods in London, but nothing compared to the leisurely perusal of frocks and other clothing items in an American department store. I needed so much and was embarrassed to have Catherine see my shabby underthings, but she told me she had always wanted to shop with a daughter and was enjoying the afternoon as much as I. We consulted companionably and for the first time I felt I was growing closer to her. It was an afternoon to delight the heart of any woman, especially one who hadn't seen such fashionable clothing for five years.

Geraldine and I were finishing breakfast the next morning when I heard a knock at the door and, at Geraldine's request, I opened it to see Janet standing there with a little boy about Johnny's age. She greeted me with that typical American "Hi," and entered saying "I told Geraldine I'd stop around this week with Bobby so the boys could meet. I figured Johnny hadn't had a chance to get to know many kids yet," continuing with an invitation for my son to join the play group the faculty wives had formed. "We take turns minding them and organizing activities," she told me. "We all hope you'll join us."

I was pleased at the invitation and told her so, feeling slightly guilty at my curiosity about Dan and her in the past. She was one of the many townspeople who had gone out of their way to be friendly and welcoming and suddenly I realized we would probably become good friends. She was easy and outgoing and I felt an affinity that I had not discerned at our first meeting.

Geraldine, still lingering over her coffee, informed me that Dan and Janet had been playmates before they attended school. With this bit of information, she gathered up the morning papers and told me she would be out for the morning. "You two get acquainted while the boys play," she suggested and quickly disappeared.

Bobby had brought over a bunch of small trucks and cars and both boys were busily engaged in transportation problems, with accompanying sounds, in the corner of the kitchen, much too busy at that point to stop for juice, another American product to marvel at, quick-frozen and needing only to be diluted with water to serve as a beverage. I hadn't crossed a threshold into another world since I left England.

How, I questioned, had Janet become a Professor of Anthropology at such a young age? It seemed like a challenging field for a woman.

"I'm only an associate professor," she explained, "but I was fortunate—the war gave me an opportunity. It was a discipline mostly dominated by men, and I was available when the college discovered their lack of candidates." I felt pity when she went on to explain that her husband had died on the second day of the landing at Omaha Beach and that teaching had been a godsent, the only way she could keep her sanity.

Dark-haired, tall, exceedingly slim, almost gangly, she wasn't pretty but an expressive face and the humor evident in her wry smile and manner of speaking held my attention and interest. She held her head cocked to one side like a bird as she spoke.

"I was here when Dan got back from England in 1940," she went on. "He told me about the girl he had loved and lost in an airplane crash. He was devastated, Joan, absolutely inconsolable. What a miracle you found each other again! Sometimes," she sighed, "It's hard for me not to resent your good fortune when I think of my husband's dying."

It was a simple statement on Janet's part, not an attempt to seek sympathy.

"Dan was good to me, Joan. We dated, but I want you to know it was never anything serious. He was kind and supportive, but we've known each other too long for any feelings of romance. He was just always there, from childhood on." I took her words at face value; perhaps that explained the bond between the two of them I sensed at first meeting.

Chapter Seventeen

Christmas was lovely with a tree decorated with shining prewar ornaments. Dinner was that American favorite, turkey, though I would have liked roast beef and Yorkshire pudding. Dan and I struggled to stuff the bird and I made a steamed pudding from memory. We relaxed during the week and I looked forward to a small New Year's Eve party at one of the faculty member's home. I was beginning to realize we were in a sort of closed circle, but enjoyed the company of the younger faculty members we met.

No one drank heavily; we played a few nonsensical games which were fun; someone commented that it was the best New Years because it was the first one we could celebrate after the war. We speculated about what 1946 would bring.

I glanced around, looking for Dan, wanting to be with him at midnight, and sought him out. I found him in the kitchen with Janet's arms around him, holding tight. I could see what I perceived to be longing in her face. Dan's face was hidden, all I could see was the back of his head bowed over hers. I may have moaned, or gasped and they broke apart, turning toward me.

Suddenly I was filled with fury, absolute rage. I couldn't speak—I couldn't cry—I couldn't believe what I had seen. As they moved toward me, I wheeled around and marched into the bedroom to find my coat and handbag. As I grasped my keys Dan came in, a horrified look on his face. I ignored his outstretched arm and his attempt at an explanation. I simply walked out and climbed into his precious Packard, tempted to smash it into a tree, except I knew I'd be injured or killed and Johnny would likely have no one to care for him.

`I drove around aimlessly. It was perhaps an hour later when I turned into the driveway of our home, shut the engine off and sat there, desolate and afraid. Why had I ever agreed to come to America? Why was I foolish enough to believe Dan loved me? How could I have been so deceived and betrayed? I entered the house, not bothering to turn on the hall light, intending to go upstairs and pack clothing for Johnny and I and seek shelter for us in a hotel somewhere.

It was Janet's voice I heard first, calling my name from the darkened living room. I turned away. Then, out of the darkness I felt Dan's arms around me and I tried to twist away. I know I cried out telling him to let me go, that I never wanted to see him again, when he brought me around to face him.

"Listen to me!" he commanded in a tone he had never used before. "Listen to both of us, Joan. We aren't lovers. We never meant you to be hurt."

"You never meant me to see or know, you mean! I don't want any explanations! I'm leaving you."

"If you won't listen to Dan, you'll have to hear me out," Janet's voice said calmly. "My husband and I were married on New Year's Eve 1941. Dan was our best man. He was holding me because I was crying, not because we were kissing. He knew how badly I felt. He was with me last New Year's Eve, too, Joan, and for many when we were children and adolescents. There's nothing else to it, Joan. We've both told you we've been friends forever. You must believe us."

I looked at both of them in the dim light entering the hallway from the street, saw the sincerity in their faces and anxiety as to whether I would accept their assurances and believe them. Slowly my wrath faded, and as I look back now, I know it was one more manifestation of my anxious attempts to adjust to my new life. I nodded, telling them I accepted their statements. I wasn't sure I really believed them, but I was willing to try.

"I'll take Janet home," Dan called up when I reached the second floor landing. "I'll be right back." In the back of my mind I realized he had already taken the babysitter home.

"Fine." At that point all I wanted to do was reach our bedroom and cry—but not before the two of them. If Dan didn't love me, I was determined he would at least have to respect me.

I was pretending to be asleep when he got back, less then ten minutes later. I heard him sigh, the clink of change and the

101

contents of his pants pockets as he placed items on his bureau, a rustle as he got undressed and went into the bathroom for his pajamas, and I lay rigid as he got into bed. I didn't respond when he drew me close, not trusting myself not to rail at him again, and afraid that we would wake Johnny up if we talked.

We had been married less than three months. It was impossible not to respond to his caresses. He kept murmuring, "I'm sorry, I'm so sorry, Joan," as he drew me tight and soon I was lost in desire and ardent response to his love-making.

Afterwards he told me the year before, both of them lonely and Janet frantic in her agony over the loss of her husband, they had thought about going to bed. "We just couldn't do it," my husband confessed. "We had known each other too long, too well—we got as far as the bedroom, turned out the light then— we realized it was impossible to continue. Janet said it would be incest as far as she was concerned, and she was right. Joan, please, believe us. Neither of us would ever want to hurt you and you know how much I love you. It was just—lousy timing."

I sighed, turning to nuzzle his chest, brush my lips across the hair tracing a path down the center of his body, press close to assure him and myself that I accepted his explanation. I had overreacted, I knew that, but deep inside me I was still hurt that they could accept their intimacy as perfectly permissible. I knew, though, that I would either have to regard their friendship as a given, or make myself miserable for the rest of my life wondering about their actions, past and present. I finally told Dan I was sorry for my outburst, but he must have realized my secret reservations.

"It will never happen again," he assured me. And, as far as I know, it never did. I fell asleep, head cradled against him, listening to the beat of his heart, as strong, steady and true as I hoped him to be.

Since then, Janet became my friend, my confidant, my support and, when necessary, my critic. She could understand the things that worried me far better than Dan and could listen with sympathy to my worries which grew less as time went on, but caused me great anxiety in the first few months of my marriage. She managed to bridge the distance I felt between faculty and faculty wife and we both laughed together over some of the other-worldly attitudes of those in Academia, especially the older professors who were still struggling to accept the post-war world.

"It's going to be difficult for them," Janet commented "when we are besieged with returning veterans who aren't going to be interested in much other than getting their degrees as fast as possible so they can get a better job. College will be the means to the end, not the end in itself. We won't see a great number of scholars, I don't think." I had heard Dan say the same thing. Probably they had discussed it many times before I came on the scene.

Occasionally I would see sadness in her eyes and berate myself for the scene I had caused New Year's Eve. I had Dan as husband and lover; she had no one to turn to but us as friends and I tried never to begrudge her the few times she asked us for advice or the instances when Dan was needed for a chore. The two boys were playmates and he selflessly tried to serve as father to Bobby, too.

So our lives began to settle into the pattern of the college semesters, intersessions and summer vacation. I grew more familiar with American customs; I watched Johnny grow in confidence and become a noisy, happy American child; I volunteered to help at school functions. I joined the Faculty Wives Club where I was a novelty for a while with my English accent, but I was reticent about how I met Dan. I felt I was still bound by the Official Secrets Act, but the few secrets I possessed surely would not have been of interest to anyone except, perhaps, a history scholar like Dan—and he knew the restrictions placed upon me.

Janet and I were both concerned about the increase in population on the campus by the return of the G.I.s. There was no more room for veteran's housing on public property. There were only a dozen or so apartments on campus designated for faculty use, and those were mostly studio apartments, so we set out to try and welcome the young mothers and children who accompanied their husbands. Although the government provided a $50 per month allowance in the beginning, it had to be raised to $90 and the families were barely able to exist. I wondered aloud why the college could not purchase trailers to house the families and Janet and I were both very active in the effort to convince the powers-to-be this would be a sensible solution. Student families finally paid $27.50 a month to rent these meagre accommodations, but it did provide shelter and the young husbands could escape the din of family life in crowded quarters by studying in the library.

I would hear Dan talking to Johnny sometimes when I was busy around the house, telling him in simple terms of America's history and her connection to England. Johnny seemed to remember much of his life in England for the first few months, then it faded away. When we returned in the summer of 1947 for the final research Dan needed to complete his thesis, he could not recall living in our old cottage. Catherine was ecstatic to see the boy, kissed me with pleasure and greeted Dan like a returning son.

The commute Dan had to make to London was too long on a daily basis and finally I asked my aunt if we could use her apartment while she was overseas with her husband. We had the place to ourselves for a month and Dan was able to acquire the necessary information he needed. Catherine offered to keep Johnny for us while we were in the City, so it was almost like a second honeymoon—well, we never had a first honeymoon.

We both looked at each other when we got ready for bed the first night. I knew our thoughts were the same: Remembering the breathless passion we shared in wartorn London, the sound of air raid sirens in the distance, the darkness of the streets and our frantic, impassioned embraces, hands seeking to touch and memorize the curves, textures, smell of each other's bodies, the sense of urgency as we kissed and abandoned ourselves to seeking, joyous satisfaction. I hadn't forgotten: I had relived it a thousand times during the nights I yearned for Dan, lying sleepless next to John. Dan's eyes were dark with desire as I glanced at him across the bed and I knew he remembered too. Our love making was more restrained, but sweet and tender, a lovely encore of our first night together. We fell asleep, curled up together, this time with the happy knowledge that unlike that time so long ago, we would be together from now on.

London was rebuilding, but it was a long process. So much had been destroyed. St. Paul's had been saved, the jewel at the heart of the city, but other landmarks were gone, or in the process of being reconstructed. Dan spent his days in research, I spent my days trying to find things Catherine had been unable to obtain. I wondered if life would ever be normal again, but knew that the old life before the war was now only a memory. England would re-build, but she would never be the world power she was, the ruler of a mighty empire. All that was lost in the fight against Hitler. The Allies had triumphed, but at a terrible cost to Great Britain. America was now the supreme world power, along with Russia, a menacing force that breathed terror over the eastern part of the continent.

"We fought a war only to give birth to a monster," Dan commented. "All that material we gave Russia is being stockpiled to use against us. Mark my words, it's going to be an uneasy next fifty or so years."

I knew his concern, but my thoughts were selfish. We had done our best, we had fought our war, whatever was to come would have to be someone else's effort. Then I shivered as I thought of Johnny. Would he have to take part in some future struggle with weapons of destruction inconceivable to us in 1939?

We flew back to the States at the end of August and Johnny entered first grade in the American public school system (Dan explained to me that the meaning was different in the United States) it wasn't Eton he would be attending but an elementary school within four blocks of our home, able to come home for lunch, dismissed at three o'clock, with time for outdoor play with Bobby.

It had taken some time for me to become reconciled to the belief that Janet and Dan were really just friends. They commiserated over classes, faculty shortcomings, edicts from Administration, and the challenge returning G.I.s presented to the classroom. These were goal-focused young men, anxious to get their degree, not interested in esoteric discussions, nor were they particularly interested in history. Why should they be, I wondered. They knew they had been part of it and their lives would be changed because of their participation. I knew Dan tried to infuse into lectures his belief that past history played a major role in any society and that the lessons learned, if heeded, could prevent the ever-repetitious cycle of economic decline, war and oppression.

"We have to learn this, make it part of our national conscience," he would say to me at times, but I knew he himself doubted if many of his students listened. I agreed with him, like any good wife, but privately put his concerns in the back of my mind. I was to busy concentrating on keeping our everyday existence running smoothly and at the end of September, two years after we found each other, I told him I was pregnant. He was happy, but raised his eyebrows and said, "I thought we had decided to wait awhile."

"We did wait awhile," I informed him. "Same problem as in 1940—no discipline, no restraint. Or else," I smiled, "it was Auntie's four-poster bed."

"Probably the bed," he agreed, holding me close, drawing back to press his lips gently against my closed eyelids, my surprising, secret erotic spot. My arms wrapped around him as he held me close. This time he would be with me and there would be no need for secret tears of longing in the night. I sighed with supreme contentment.

I told Janet the next day, watching closely for her reaction. Try as I might, I could never entirely obliterate that New Year's Eve from my memory. "I envy you," she said quietly. "I'll never be able to say that. I'm lucky I have Bobby—Jim didn't want me to get pregnant while he was away. He said we should wait until he got back. But I couldn't wait. Somehow I knew I had to conceive a child, just in case—and I was right, wasn't I?" I saw the look on her face and knew at that minute she felt exactly the way I had when I thought I had lost Dan, thankful that I carried his child beneath my heart. "I know, Janet, I know. That's the way I felt with Johnny." She looked at me in puzzled surprise and I realized I had never told her who Johnny's father was. "He was conceived the night before Dan returned in 1940. I married another man, a good man, who accepted the fact it was not his child, but I was always grateful for my baby."

Janet hesitated, then stated, "Dan loved you beyond belief, Joan. When I got word Jim died, Dan sat and cried with me, too. He told me about your meeting—I don't think he would have ever married. Joan, believe me, we shared good times as kids, but our bond was the loss of the people we loved most in the world." She reached over to hug me and whispered, "I'm so happy for both of you." I knew if the situations had been reversed, I never could have been so magnanimous. I would have been consumed with bitter envy.

In spite of my fears, I grew to love America and the academic life we enjoyed in Brentley. Johnny adjusted well, he adored all things American and accepted Dan as his father, although we delayed explanations until he was older. I knew I would always be the English woman Professor Childress married, but made every effort to adapt to American customs and outlook.

At twelve Johnny was beginning to question and challenge some of his father's statements and theories and their exchanges were sometimes heated, though Dan made it a point to listen carefully, thoughtfully to his son's viewpoint. We both recognized an independence of mind we hoped could be channeled into a potential scholar.

Dan, thirty-eight, had matured into a distinguished, prematurely grey-haired academician, well-published, well-recognized in his field of Twentieth Century American studies and I was comfortable in my role of supportive faculty wife. Our moments of high passion were far less frequent, though his touch never failed to stir me. We had been so fortunate. Our love for each other had deepened and matured with our marriage in spite of our mutually perceived differences, differences we strove to reconcile through the years.

There were times I studied my husband's face and thought back on our first meeting, over a decade ago, and our precipitous adventures together in the world of espionage. Time cast a veil over the dangers we had shared, and if I dwelt on those moments of tension and high excitement, it was to wonder that we had experienced such terror and heightened surges of adrenalin. I was simply grateful for the miracle that brought us back together.

In l952 Guardian College decided to participate in a dialogue between American and European institutions of higher learning. Dan was enthusiastic about the possibilities involved, commenting it was a chance to see if the wounds of war could be healed by a mutual exchange of research and information. By this time he was a candidate for the Dean of the College of Liberal Arts.

The first speaker would be an academician from West Germany, a Dieter Hoffmeyer, whose comments about Nazi Germany and its effects on the traditional outlook of the German people were recognized in academic circles worldwide, especially by Dan who cited him several times in his articles published in scholarly journals. Hoffmeyer had recently emerged from obscurity, and his growing fame had interested even me, never a scholarly type. I planned to accompany Dan to the reception planned in his honor after his lecture.

"Have you gotten past the point of hating anything German?" Dan asked as I dressed that evening.

I shrugged, nodded yes and commented, "I never hated Germans as a whole, but I can't forget or forgive the terror I went through in the labor camp, But they were Hitler's men, not civilians, I realize that now." I leaned forward to mascara my lashes and study my face to see if I needed rouge. Maybe a touch. It was evening and I was wearing a black, low-necked dinner gown. I smiled with pleasure as Dan leaned down to kiss the exposed hollow above my collarbones, caressing him lightly on his cheek as he did so.

It was late. Dan's shirt studs had to be fastened and cufflinks inserted into his shirt sleeves. I shook my head wondering why only women could manage these details, knowing it was because Dan loved the attention I provided. I meant to tell him about the cablegram I received that afternoon from Colonel Jenkins, a surprise indeed, cautioning me to be aware of any attempt to contact me by German nationals.

I had not heard from British Intelligence for years, not since we married and I had formally applied for American citizenship. Who, I wondered, would have the least bit of interest in me after all this time? They could not have meant Hoffmeyer, I was certain.

It never occurred to me to think of Dieter, the man Dan and I had testified against at Nuremberg—that is, not until the last minute when I realized the first names were identical. The report my General Barclay had referred to when we landed in England was available only on a need-to-know basis. Frowning, I reached to the top of my closet where I kept a small revolver, issued to me years ago by British Intelligence. It was not accurate at more than twenty feet, but at close range could kill or severely wound. My fingers groped for the ammunition kept in a hat box at the rear of the top shelf. While Dan finished dressing I slipped the gun into my evening bag, creating a bulge, so much so that I had to remove my compact and change purse, neither of which were essential, but which, out of habit, I carried. I remember thinking the items I extracted were the ones I would need, surely not the gun. "It's all coincidence anyway," I murmured to myself, shaking my head when Dan asked me what I said.

When Dieter approached the podium after his introduction by the college president Dan and I drew in our breaths sharply, looking at one another with dismay. It was the same man who had betrayed us, so many years ago. He had been sentenced to five years in prison; probably released before his sentence was up, like so many minor war criminals whose excuse, invariably, was they were only doing what they were told to do by their leaders.

Dieter's speech was well-rehearsed, well-thought out, logical in its presentation and compelling in its summary, a not too subtle plea for understanding and forgiveness for the sins of the official Nazi regime. I listened to him in anger, remembering his success in taking the professor away from us, and the resultant horror I had experienced when I had to bring the physicist out of the camp. Would he recognize me? And, if so, what would his actions be?

There was not the slightest hint of recognition when we were both introduced at the reception. He complimented Dan on some article he had written, bowed low over my hand to kiss it in that continental manner, and told us how pleased he was to be in America.

"We are hoping," he said pompously, "that the wounds of war are healing for both our countries and that East and West Germany can be united once again."

I smiled at him and thought to myself, "Not as long as I live, I hope." The specter of a reunited Germany terrified me.

Dieter had brought his wife with him, a tall blond with generously endowed bosoms, and an accent I could scarcely understand. Dan offered his arm to escort her to the buffet and I found myself with my arm on Dieter's, trying not to shudder at his touch. The man was evil: I still felt it, along with rage he was a free man. I was silent, not even attempting casual conversation. He followed behind me as I picked up a few items from the surprisingly wide selection the college had provided, wondering why they had gone all-out for a recent enemy.

Undoubtedly the college did not have the animosity I held toward our former enemies.

I felt Dieter's eyes on my back as I proceeded through the line, walking across the room to stand by Dieter's wife and Dan who was watching us both intently. As I took my place beside my husband I turned to Dieter and, knowing I wanted no one else to see my agitation, asked politely if he was enjoying his stay in the States. I met his gaze firmly, waiting for his reply.

"It's good to see old friends and acquaintances," he replied. His accent was good, his English grammatical. He added, "I've enjoyed talking to your husband whose observations on current history surprised and enlightened me. I don't agree, but then, we have completely different perspectives, do we not?" I felt he included me in his question, though his eyes were on Dan.

"We certainly come from different backgrounds, different experiences," Dan agreed. "Do you find much resentment in your travels as a German representing your country?" I knew Dan was deliberately challenging Dieter, probing to see what his intent was, whether he represented any danger to us, difficult to believe at that point in time.

"Only just now." He turned to speak to me. The scar I remembered from years ago was still a faint mark across his upper cheek, his blue eyes held mine, a slight smile on his thin-lipped mouth. "Tell me, Mrs. Childress, after your successful escape from our labor camp with Professor Aubuchon—" I drew in my breath sharply "were you sent on any further missions? Somehow your name never arose again in our files, nor did your husband's"

"No, I was very ill when I returned to England and I resigned from the service. My war efforts after that were minimal." I would have never revealed the actions British Intelligence took to conceal our identifies, heartless as they seemed to me at the time.

"I imagine your exodus from camp was horrific," Dieter continued, tantalizing me with his knowledge. Suddenly I realized he knew the whole story and wondered why he hadn't prevented the operation from succeeding. Or, was he there to oversee it, I suddenly wondered. Aloud, I replied with a shudder, "It was the worst experience of my life. I still have nightmares about it." The moment I said this I wished I had not revealed my weakness.

"It was the only way we could get you out," Dieter explained, a note of sympathy in his voice and I realized at that moment he was what he seemed to be in 1940 when we were trying to reach the airfield. He was a double agent, serving Britain and at the same time a Nazi informer.

"But it was you who took the Professor from us. Dan and I both testified against you at Nuremberg. You were imprisoned, I thought, for five years. Why didn't you defend yourself? Why didn't you prove your identify as a British agent? I never saw you at that camp—I would have remembered you; I would have known you." I would have been incapable of action, I thought grimly, if I had known you were there, so frightened was I of you.

"I had to make a quick decision that night in France," Dieter explained. "I was suspect. I knew how important Professor Aubuchon was to the Allies—he was doubly important to the Nazis. He was an expert on heavy water which Germany used to try to split the atom. If Aubuchon had gotten away it would have discredited me and I knew he could be rescued from the camp with my intervention at a later date. I let you and your husband escape knowing you, Mrs. Childress, could come back and contact the professor later. With help from me as the liaison between the camp commandant and Berlin, the means for escape could be arranged."

"But you willingly went to prison after the war. Why?"

"It was Colonel Barclay's successor's idea. It provided cover for me and I could make contact with German communists who were plotting to gain control after the Allied occupation. I stayed only four months, then my sentence was commuted."

I felt the weight of the little revolver in my evening purse as I gazed at him. He knew all the names, his explanations were impeccable and I suddenly realized I believed him. He had been an unseen ally, setting up the whole escape from the camp. I had never been told any information about my contact. Someone had entered my barracks late at night, whispered the plan in my ear and told me it would take place the next evening. I realized the only-need-to-know basis had protected all of us at the time. I don't think it was Dieter who spoke to me in the dark that night: It was one of his underlings.

Dan and I were silent for a minute or two, absorbing all Dieter had told us, then my husband asked, "Where will you go from here?"

"Stamford," he told us. "Then, back to Germany. I really am a scholar," he asserted with a smile. "I knew you were here at Guardian," indicating Dan, "and I wanted to see both of you to try to explain my actions."

"I thought you might be seeking revenge for our testimony," I admitted.

He shook his head. "We do what we have to do at the time. I do have one question though, Mrs. Childress."

I raised my eyebrows. "What's that?"

"I learned later you were pregnant when you left the camp. Was your child born? I worried about that. I told General Barclay I thought it was heartless to submit you to such a mission in your condition."

"I didn't realize I was pregnant when I agreed. Yes, I had a little boy. He's twelve now. I also have a daughter. How did you know about my pregnancy?"

"The General told me before he died. He said you were one of the bravest women he ever met."

High praise indeed from a man who displayed no sentiment, never faltered in his efforts to carry out his assigned mission, gave me little or no indication whether I had done well or poorly in my efforts and, with the exception of his kind treatment of us when Dan and I landed from France, treated me more like a not-too-bright servant than a competent operative.

We had nothing further to discuss. The final chapter was written, seven years after the war. Dieter clicked his heels, bowed, turned and walked over to the college president to say goodbye. Dan and I looked at each other.

"Do you believe him?" I questioned.

He shrugged his shoulders dismissively. "It doesn't matter now. He's no threat to us. But I find it hard to believe the scholarly works I've been reading were written by someone we both feared and despised."

I was in agreement. "I never would have had Johnny, Dan, if he hadn't been able to get us out. I guess I owe him a debt of gratitude for that, but I wonder why I received this cable today?" I opened my purse and showed him the warning cablegram.

That question was to remain unanswered forever.

About the Author

With a background in advertising, public relations, journalism, and free-lance writing, Erica Kinsey has been published in *Industry* magazine and *Trailer Life*, as well as columns on crafts, gardening, and cooking for local New England newspapers.

She holds a BA in English Literature from Fairleigh Dickinson University in Madison, New Jersey. Currently she is working on a novel about life in a New England mill town and its effect on a young minister and a young woman he befriends.

Born in New Jersey, Erica resided in Massachusetts for a number of years and has recently made her home in Central Florida. She credits her oldest son, always fascinated with World War II, with the inspiration to write this book.

Ms. Kinsey lists swimming and reading as her favorite pastimes and is an avid fan of PBS British comedies.

Printed in the United States
3934